CHRISTMAS WISH

JILL SANDERS

GRAYTON

DIGITAL ISBN: 978-1-945100-20-8

PRINT ISBN: 9798652617295

IS PRINT ISBN: 978-1-945100-28-4

Copyeditor: Erica Ellis – inkdeepediting.com

SUMMARY

Laura's been down on her luck with love, starting with Simon Berg. After the man of her fantasies left her shattered years ago, she determined to never let anyone get close to her again. She would have succeeded if Simon hadn't waltzed back into her life a month before Christmas.

Leaving Laura had been the hardest thing Simon had ever had to do, but it had been the only way to save her from the hell that was surrounding him. But now that he's made a name for himself and escaped the horrors of his past, he can finally focus on winning back the only woman he has ever loved.

PROLOGUE

*E*ven though Laura was only ten years old, she understood why she, her brother, and her mother were moving into the small two-bedroom apartment that sat directly over the complex's laundry room.

Divorce. It was something several of her friends had talked about. Her older brother Logan had explained it to her in his not-so-subtle way.

Her parents were no longer going to be a family. And that was just fine by her. She knew the hell her father had put Logan through. It seemed that every chance he could, their father was hitting Logan for one reason or another.

Even though her father had never raised a hand to her, she had felt every slap, every push, every terrible name her father had called her brother just the same. After all, Logan was the only person she'd ever looked up to. The only one she'd ever loved unconditionally. No, even her mother hadn't earned that from her. Yet.

Gina Miller was spineless and a coward, in Laura's ten-year-old mind. It was strange—the woman acted as if she was the one taking the abuse, when, in fact, Laura's father had never lifted a hand or raised his voice to his wife. He reserved that for his son.

A mother was supposed to protect her son. Not only did she not rise up to defend him, she at times looked the other way and once even left in the middle of a bad incident that had left Logan with a bloody lip and a bruised cheek.

Both Laura and her brother were looking forward to the new life. To starting over and forgetting the horrors of their past.

At first, Logan continued to act out, as he had when they had lived in Golden under their father's rules. Then he'd settled into finding himself, a man who stood up for the weak and defended others against bullies like their father. Even their mother changed and started coming out of her shell, as she called it.

Laura, on the other hand, took years before she opened up and trusted someone other than Logan.

Then she'd met Simon Berg at her new school in Cherry Creek. It had taken her several years for her to trust Simon, but he'd been there, patiently waiting the entire time as their friendship blossomed and grew into true love. Then, everything had been perfect.

So when Simon up and disappeared on her just before their graduation, she'd been left more than just brokenhearted. She'd turned angry and bitter at every man in the world.

CHAPTER 1

*L*aura was running late for work, again. She hated Mondays. Absolutely freaking hated them. It had been two years since she'd moved back to Golden, Colorado, to take a job at her brother's new business. Well, okay, it was technically her uncle's old business, which he'd handed over for her brother and his wife Amy to run together.

Logan and Laura's uncle, Gary, had finally retired and left Rocky Mountain Real Estate to the newlyweds. One of the first things they had done was to snag Laura from Cherry Creek Realty, a job she'd gotten fresh out of high school. She'd quickly worked her way up in that company while taking night classes. She was thankful that her brother had hired her on as head of RMR's interior design division to oversee small renovations, stage furniture and artwork, and take care of other small details so that homes or businesses could be made ready for the best possible sales price.

She loved her work but hated Mondays. Anything and everything that could go wrong usually happened to her on Mondays.

That morning, she'd almost left her apartment with two different shoes on. Thankfully, she'd caught her error the moment she'd stepped outside into the deep snow, as one heeled boot sunk into the depths of the cold snow while the other, the higher boot with the spiky heel, kept her foot dry and warm.

She'd rushed back inside, and it had taken her almost ten minutes to find the correct boot, which of course made her late and left her apartment in total disarray. She'd planned on stopping off at the little coffee shop on the corner for some hot cinnamon rolls and the delicious spiced coffee she liked so much but now that she was late, she had to settle for a smashed granola bar that had been sitting at the bottom of her purse and wash it down with the tasteless bland coffee from the office kitchen.

Sure enough, while she hunted in the fridge for some creamer, she spilled someone's leftover spaghetti lunch all over her pants.

By the time she'd cleaned herself up, her coffee was cold, and she was in an even fouler mood. Sitting at her desk, Beverly, a new temp she had been working with, gave her a look.

"What?" She groaned. "I know I'm late."

"Nothing." Beverly smiled at her. Beverly had worked at RMR for almost six months. She was the third temp Laura had gone through since being there. She hadn't had issues with the first two, but both had decided to move on to greener pastures. So far, Beverly appeared happy with the position and fit in better at RMR than the previous two people.

Laura liked Beverly. The woman was almost twice Laura's age but was in better shape than she was. She knew that Beverly attended yoga classes four times a week and, on the weekends, went biking or hiking with her boyfriend, a man half her age.

"Looks like someone got out of bed on the wrong side?" Beverly murmured.

"I think I used up all my luck getting out of bed this morning without breaking anything," she replied as she turned on her computer.

Just as the thing booted up, Logan poked his head in the office she shared with Beverly.

"Hey, heads-up. I need you in this meeting that starts now." He looked at his watch and, before she could reply, he disappeared.

"Meeting?" She frowned. "What meeting?" she asked Beverly, who just shrugged.

If her computer were faster, she would have had time to glance at the schedule, but since it was taking its sweet time, she grabbed her cold coffee and rushed down the hallway to the large meeting room.

When she stepped inside, she was shocked to see her brother shaking the hand of a man she thought she'd never see—or forgive—ever again.

She almost turned around and left, but her brother called to her and waved her into the room.

"Laura, there you are." Logan moved over and took her by the shoulders when she didn't move out of the doorway.

It was as if her entire body had frozen up. As her brother nudged her forward, her legs were so stiff that she almost tripped on the spiky heels of her boots.

She normally wasn't a vain woman, but still she had dreamed of the moment she would see Simon Berg again so many times over the years. None of them entailed her wearing the outfit she currently had on, complete with the new spaghetti stain on her left knee.

Damn, why did he have to look so perfect? He looked even better than the last time she'd seen him. His jet-black hair was longer, the way she'd always liked it. He even looked taller than when he'd left five years ago. Taller and more muscular than he had been last time, she noticed as she got closer.

"Simon's back! Isn't this great?" Logan nudged her closer to the man she'd dreamed of for the past five years.

"It's good to see you again, Laura," Simon said as his eyes ran over her.

She felt her entire body vibrate under his gaze. Looking down at his outstretched hands, she was finally able to get her mind in gear.

As if it didn't belong to her, her arm raised up and poured her cold coffee over Simon's head. With pleasure racing through her, she smiled as the coffee caused his styled hair to fall in his eyes. She noticed a smile flash on his lips before she jerked away and stormed out of the room.

She didn't stop until she stood out on the employees' balcony at the back of the old building. She wrapped her arms around herself and desperately wished she'd thought to stop off at her desk for her coat.

"Want to tell me what that was all about?" Logan said, stepping onto the balcony and wrapping his jacket around her shoulders.

"No," she bit back at her brother.

"Fine." He leaned on the railing and looked out over the mountains. "Amy's having to tap dance in there."

Suddenly, she realized that there could be consequences to her actions. Had Simon been a big client? Had she just lost her brother's business a lot of money? Could Simon sue the company?

"Shit," she groaned. "I didn't think. I'm sorry." She leaned on the railing next to her brother. She'd been so upset about seeing Simon again that she hadn't thought. She wasn't even taking in the beautiful view of the snow-covered mountains sitting directly in front of her.

"Amy's a pro at fixing situations like this." Logan nudged her shoulder. "Want to talk about it?"

She glared at her brother as she turned towards him. "He up and left me. Left us," she said with a frown. "No explanation. No note. No goodbye."

"And for that, I'll be forever sorry," a deep voice said from the doorway.

They both turned as Simon stepped out onto the deck.

"I'll..." Her brother glanced towards the building and, without saying anything, left them alone.

"Coward," she groaned at her brother's back as Simon moved over and stood next to her.

She noticed his hair was back to being perfect and looked even better slicked back from his perfect face. The new style accented his chiseled features and his haunting blue eyes even further.

She turned away from the man who had not only broken her heart, but broken her, completely.

"What do you want?" she asked between clenched teeth.

"To apologize," Simon surprised her by saying.

She spared him a glance. "I'm the one that dumped coffee over your head."

"I'm just thankful it was cold," he said with a chuckle. He'd always been good at avoiding answering questions. When she'd been younger, she'd fallen for the broody dark boy. Now, however, she was having none of it.

"What are you doing here?" She turned to him and tried to ignore how handsome he was.

"If you'd come back into the meeting room, you'd find out," he said easily.

She tilted her head slightly and gave him a look that said she wasn't going to go along with his games.

"Nice place," he said with a nod to the building behind them. "Have you been working here long?"

She figured two could play at his game.

Her eyes narrowed as she asked, "Something tells me you've known all along that I worked here with my brother. And for how long."

He turned and glanced off at the view of the mountains. When she visibly shivered and hugged her brother's jacket closer to her, he said, "Come inside. You're freezing."

Without replying, she marched towards the door. She was only going inside because she was cold. Just yesterday she'd been wearing short sleeves and open-toe shoes to work. The snow and chill had crept in during the night and, according to the weather reports, would be sticking around through New Year's Day.

She felt Simon follow her inside and for a brief moment dreamed of slamming the door in his face and leaving him locked out in the cold. Then she noticed her brother and Amy waiting for them just outside the conference room, and she lifted her chin, determined to get through the meeting for their sake.

"Shall we try this again?" Amy asked in a cheery voice.

Laura held in a low groan as she passed her brother and sister-in-law. In the few years that her brother and Amy had been married, Laura and Amy had grown into more than friends. They acted just like sisters at this point. Laura really liked Amy.

As everyone settled in the conference room, Laura realized that the man was throwing her completely off. For some reason, she couldn't wrap her mind around anything that anyone was saying. Especially after the conference room had filled with every employee at RMR. When her brother had started to explain how RMR was partnering with a company called ReVision Development on a big project, she assumed that Simon worked for the other firm and was there for the partnership.

Logan explained that the project would be a six-week-long

ordeal. To her utter shock, Logan turned to her and told her that she had been chosen to work one-on-one with ReVision Development's liaison to ensure the project went smoothly. And of course, with her outstanding Monday luck, that liaison was Simon Berg.

CHAPTER 2

Simon couldn't keep his eyes or his mind focused on anything other than Laura. How long had it been since he'd been in the same room as her?

Too long. It hadn't been safe until now.

Just sitting in a room full of people he felt comfortable being around was something he hadn't done in a long time. Even now, his entire body remained on guard, his back to a wall and the door in his peripheral vision.

His main focus, of course, was solely on the woman of his dreams. The woman he was determined to win back as quickly as possible. The one he should have never let go in the first place.

"So, it's settled," Logan Miller, Laura's older brother, finished saying. Back in the day, Logan had been like an older brother to Simon. He'd felt like the Millers—Logan, Laura, and their mother, Gina—had allowed him into their little family. Then everything had changed when he'd ruined everything. "Beverly will move into the annex so you can make room for Simon in your office."

His eyes focused on Laura's and could immediately see the anger behind them.

"I don't think—" she began, only to have her brother wave her unvoiced concerns away.

"We can discuss the final details later," her brother said quickly. "I think we're all eager to get back to work." He dismissed everyone. Immediately, people jumped up from their chairs and started moving out of the conference room.

Laura rushed over to her brother and—he could tell by the face she was making—scolded him quietly.

Pasting on an easy smile, Simon walked over to shake Logan's hand.

"That was enlightening," he admitted, his eyes moving to Laura's. "I'm looking forward to working with you."

"Go to hell," she said under her breath.

"Excuse me?" he asked easily with a smile.

"I think what my sister was saying"—Logan stepped in front of Laura—"is that it's going to be a pleasure working with ReVision Development." Logan stepped back and wrapped an arm tightly around his sister's shoulders.

Simon smiled bigger as Laura narrowed her eyes at him.

"If you need anything," Amy Miller, Logan's wife interjected, "our offices are on the top floor." She beamed. He'd had a conference call with the couple last week to work out some of the finer details of the partnership. But this was the first time he'd met Amy Miller. He could tell instantly that he'd like the pretty blonde woman and that she was completely devoted to Logan and the business.

It had been pure luck that he'd stumbled across the old article about their marriage online last year. It had taken him a few more months to put his plan in motion. He'd had his secretary use the company to find just what he needed for the project of his lifelong dreams.

Now that everything was finally in place, his main mission

in life was to win Laura back. To prove to her that he wasn't the flake she believed him to be. That it had been in her best interest for him to disappear all those years ago.

"If you want, I'll show you to your desk," Amy said to him.

"No." Laura nudged her brother aside and squared her shoulders. "Since I'll be working with him, I'll show him around."

Simon noticed a look cross between the siblings before he turned and followed Laura out of the conference room.

He was greeted and welcomed by a handful of other employees as Laura showed him around the three-story building used by RMR, as everyone was calling the company.

By the time they walked into Laura's office, which he would share with her, he could tell that Laura had finally brushed off the initial shock of seeing him.

The moment the office door shut behind him, she turned on him.

"I may have to work with you, but that doesn't mean I have to like it. You left me." She crossed her arms over her chest. "You left me," she repeated.

"Yes, I did," he admitted, not wanting to go into his reasons quite yet. "For now, what do you say we focus on the work?"

Her eyes narrowed slightly. Then, when he didn't say anything, she waved her hand to the smaller desk near a corner.

"Your desk." She turned and almost dismissed him as she moved to sit behind the larger desk near the picture windows.

"Nice view," he said, moving over to the windows. "You can almost see Denver from here."

"On a clear day, you can." She booted up her computer, then glanced up at him and waited, as if she was expecting him to say something further.

"I heard about your uncle retiring," he said as he leaned against the window frame.

"What did you say you do at ReVision?" she asked as her eyes ran over him.

He knew she was taking in the suit. The last time she'd seen him, he'd been dressed in worn jeans and most likely a torn T-shirt. A far cry from the attire he was wearing now, which cost him several thousand.

Removing his jacket slowly, he laid it over the back of the office chair and sat down. "This and that." He figured vagueness was necessary until he had time to let her get used to him being around again.

He smiled slightly when her eyes narrowed and the cute little twitch in her lips started up. He'd missed seeing it. Missed seeing her. How he'd forgotten the cute little hints she gave of her emotions. Currently, the twitch indicated that she was annoyed. For some odd reason, that had his smile growing.

He'd never liked seeing her that way before. Maybe because she'd never been annoyed with him before now?

Actually, when he thought about their past, she'd never been annoyed, angry, or upset at him. The entire eight years they had been best friends, sweethearts, and then lovers, she'd never been upset at him.

He was finding it oddly arousing now. He figured he'd have time enough to explore those feelings since they had the next six weeks to work with each other.

"Did you do this on purpose?" she asked, leaning back in her chair.

"What?" He mimicked her move, crossing his arms over his chest.

He held his breath as her eyes zoned in on the new muscles hiding underneath the grey dress shirt. A flash of desire flooded her eyes, and he saw her cheeks heat slightly before she jerked her chair around and faced her computer screen.

"Getting my brother to force us to work with each other?" she answered, facing away from him.

"Something tells me that, as the new owner of RMR, your brother won't be forced into anything."

"Co-owner," she threw over her shoulder.

"Right," he relented, "co-owner. So, what do you think of Amy?"

Her eyes jerked to his. "I love her. Why?"

He shrugged. "Just getting a feel for what the dynamics are around here. I always liked Logan. I guess I want to make sure he's happy."

"Very. We all are," she added, facing away from him. "So, what exactly do you need from me?" She turned back to him.

"To begin with?" He had the entire plan worked out, but sitting in the same room with her, being this close to the woman he'd dreamed about for the past five years, his carefully laid plans eluded his mind.

His eyes ran over her as she waited for his response. He'd forgotten how silvery blue her eyes were. How plump those sexy lips of hers were. For a moment, he let his memories of kissing them, of how they'd felt against his own lips, his skin, play in his mind.

"Well?" Laura asked, her voice breaking him from the trance.

Swallowing his desire, he shook his head. "I have the details here." He picked up the briefcase containing his laptop. "I know you probably have a few things of your own to tie up. What do you say we give ourselves an hour, then start on the project?" He thought about all the emails from the weekend that were probably piling up. He normally took care of them first thing Monday morning. "Maybe make that two?" he suggested.

She shrugged. "It's your time." She turned back to her computer and started working.

Turning away from her and focusing on his own tasks was the hardest thing he'd done in years. Almost as hard as leaving her in the first place five years ago.

Still, the first email he opened focused his mind on his work and quickly enough he lost himself in the task of catching up.

The small tingle he felt between his shoulder blades reminded him that she was there behind him. When his inbox was cleared and his Monday morning to-do list was finished, he turned back to watch her work.

He could see her large monitor clearly from across the room, and he watched her work her magic on designing the interior of a home.

"You have a talent," he said, causing her to jump slightly. He'd walked across the room to stand behind her and hadn't even realized he'd moved from his chair. "Sorry," he murmured.

She glanced back at him with renewed annoyance. "Thanks," she said dryly.

"I guess it's why your brother thought we'd be a good fit." He moved back a step. He watched her save the project and shut down the program.

"What exactly is the project I'll be working on? My brother didn't mention any details in the meeting."

"I can email you all of the details," he offered. She nodded quickly, so he walked over and hit send on the draft email he'd compiled a few minutes earlier.

He moved back to stand beside her as she opened the file that he'd emailed from his other, basic email account. It wasn't as if he was trying to hide who he was and what he was to the project, he just wanted her to get excited about the project for what it was. An exciting new development that would help hundreds of children and families.

A project that would, hopefully, undo all the terrible things he'd witnessed in his lifetime.

CHAPTER 3

*L*aura was slightly shocked when she opened the project file. From what she could tell, there was an extremely large old building that was being broken down into what appeared to be smaller dorm rooms. Each floor had a large kitchen, living spaces, and offices or… she zoomed in on the space.

"Are these classrooms?" she asked as she glanced back at him.

"Yes. There will be a large library, kitchen, and cafeteria on the main floor, as well as family visiting areas on the second floor. Plenty of outdoor space as well, including walking and bike pathways," he answered with a smile as his eyes ran over the screen.

She was momentarily distracted at watching the eagerness and excitement behind his eyes.

"What exactly is this project?" She turned back to the screen and tried to get a better idea of why any business would turn such a massive building into a school.

He handed her a folder. She opened it and ran her eyes over the proposed building. There was a name on the top.

"ReNewed Foster Care Facility?" She turned to him. "A foster home?" He nodded slowly and watched her. "And your employer is building it?"

"No, ReVision is funding it. The building currently exists. The old Coors warehouse just outside of town. Denver Urban Development has done all the architectural work. Construction is almost complete. That's where you come in."

"What do you need me for?" she asked, and when his eyes ran over her slowly, she felt her entire body heat. "What do you need RMR for? We do real estate. Are you looking to sell it once it's done?"

"No, you guys helped us purchase it over a year ago. Normally Kristen at Urban Development would be doing this part of the job, but she's currently out on maternity leave."

"Yes, she's best friends with Amy." Laura smiled. "I attended Kristen's baby shower last month." She remembered visiting the family just a few weeks back. Their new little girl, Jade, was just as perfect as her bigger brother, Camden.

She'd wondered when her brother and sister-in-law would start their own family, since they'd been married a little over two years now. Not that she was pushing them to have kids before they were ready. She didn't even know if they wanted kids, but she did love the idea of a niece or a nephew.

"Right." He sighed. "So, after asking around for another interior designer that would be able to finish my vision, I was told that you are one of the best in town to help me make the inside of the facility as comfortable and functional as possible."

It didn't get past her that he'd said *I* and *me*, instead of *we* or *the business*. She thought about doing a project this big. Of finally getting behind something that she could be excited about.

She remembered that Simon had grown up in the foster care system. For the first few years they'd been friends, he'd bounced between a couple homes until he'd finally settled at a facility not far from the school. Settled without a family of his own.

She touched his hand, which rested on the edge of her desk.

"How far along are they on the construction?" she asked.

"They're just finishing up." He sighed. "I'd hoped the facility would be ready to open by Christmas but without your help..." He sat on the edge of her desk and crossed his arms over his chest.

"Christmas? That's only..." She calculated how much time was left before the holiday. "Seven weeks away."

"Can you do it?" he almost challenged.

She found it difficult to keep her eyes away from the way the material stretched over the impressive muscles that he hadn't had the last time they'd been together. Her hands itched to reach out and explore them, but her mind continued to scream and remind her that this was the man who had hurt her more than anyone in her life.

She turned back to the screen and ran her mind over the importance of such a project. Of giving the kids a new home for the holidays. Her heart ached at the thought.

Not that she didn't love working for her brother, but in the few months since she'd gotten her bachelor's degree, she'd been dreaming of going off on her own. Of getting projects that she would be passionate about.

She didn't mind doing the designs for RMR. But moving around furniture to sell a home wasn't the work she desired the most. What she wanted to be doing was something important, something amazing, something worthy. Here was her chance. The fact that Simon Berg was the one bringing it to her table stung, but as she ran her eyes over the screen and the drawings of the facility, she figured she could get past all that. If it meant she would be making a mark on a project so worthy, then she could overlook the pain.

"Well?" he said after a moment. "Do you think you could have the place ready for kids to move in by then?"

She swiveled her chair and ran her eyes over him once more. His brown eyes held a hint of excitement behind them.

"Something tells me you already know the answer to that question."

His smile was quick and sexy as hell. If she'd been standing, she feared he would have knocked her on her butt with his expression. Damn.

He held out his hand for hers. She hesitated for a split second, then shook it. She hadn't counted on him holding onto it and then lifting it to his lips and kissing her knuckles.

"I meant what I said earlier," he said, his voice going lower.

"Hm?" She didn't trust her voice and wished for a glass of water to clear the knot in her throat.

"I'll be forever sorry for how I left things." His eyes searched hers.

She tensed and felt her heart drop. She had to be careful around him. Yes, she loved the idea of the project but hated the idea of working so closely with Simon. If she wasn't careful, between the looks and his smooth way of doing things, she would fall for him all over again, opening an opportunity for him to hurt her once more.

Tensing, she pulled her hand free and glanced at the screen. "I'll work the project, but anything that was between us is gone. It died when you left." She lifted her chin slightly. "I'm not the same naive girl you left behind."

"No." He smiled and stood up. "I can tell you aren't the same girl."

"As far as this goes"—she motioned between them— "we have a working relationship, nothing more. Agreed?"

He ran his hands over hers and instead of answering, nodded once.

"Good." She turned back towards her computer. "Now, I'll

need to contact someone at Denver Urban Development to get access to their updates, then I'll want to tour the facility myself."

"Aiden has set up a login for the project." He opened the folder and then rummaged through the papers he'd given her and came up with the information.

She logged into Urban Development's servers and opened the project page.

"These are great," she admitted after looking through them. "I should be able to start after lunch today."

He nodded. "How about grabbing some lunch together? We can discuss…"

She stopped him by swiveling around and giving him a look.

"I already have plans," she lied. There was no way she was going to let him get too close. Besides, she couldn't allow herself to fall into those deep eyes of his. They were her kryptonite.

His eyes searched hers, and she knew the moment he realized she was lying to him. As he leaned closer to her, a slow smile spreading on his lips, she held her breath and held her will against him.

Just then, there was a quick knock on the office door and Logan walked in.

"Hey," he said, taking in the scene quickly. "Amy wanted me to remind you about your lunch today with her. She'll meet you downstairs in ten." She was a little surprised at the news that she had a planned lunch with her sister-in-law. Then her brother's eyes moved to Simon, and she understood that Amy was playing her savior. He said to Simon, "I thought since it was your first day here, we could grab some lunch and catch up, maybe talk about some more specifics?"

Simon leaned back and nodded in agreement quickly.

"Good." Logan smiled. "I'm heading out now." He paused and glanced back at her.

Laura's eyes narrowed. No matter how much she loved her

brother, she was going to have a hard time forgiving him for springing this mess on her.

She watched concern and fear cross Logan's eyes and couldn't help but smile. Good. There was one thing she'd always made clear to her older brother. She could be vicious when it came to paybacks.

"Have a good lunch," she said sweetly and turned back to her computer to lock it so she could go find Amy.

"What was my brother thinking?" she asked when she climbed into her sister-in-law's car a few minutes later.

"I know." Amy groaned. "I figured I'd save you but was afraid Simon would see through my lies about having a scheduled lunch with you."

She touched Amy's arm. "Thanks for saving me all the same." She crossed her arms over her chest. "But I am thoroughly pissed at your husband."

"I don't blame you," Amy said as she pulled out of the parking lot. "I figured we'd head over and have tacos since Logan's taking Simon to Main Street Grill for lunch."

"Anything sounds good at this point. I missed breakfast." She felt her stomach growl at the thought of food.

"So." Amy glanced over at her. "Your brother has only vaguely mentioned Simon. You and he dated in school? How long did you two know each other?"

Laura leaned her head back and watched the snow fall outside the car window.

"Seven years. We were best friends, first then... started dating when we were fifteen," Laura answered.

"Wow." Amy shook her head. "That's a long time. What ended it?"

Laura laughed. "My brother didn't tell you that part?"

"No, I just found out this morning by watching your face when you saw Simon that you and he... had a past. I asked Logan after the meeting and he mumbled something. I think he realized how deep he had stepped in it with you after your little... display. His words, not mine," Amy added quickly.

"Yeah." She sighed and tried to clear the pain. "He left a week before graduation. No word, no note, no explanation of why or where he'd gone."

Amy frowned over at her as she parked in front of the restaurant. "You haven't seen him since? Until today?"

"Nope." She shook her head.

"What about his family? What did they say?" Amy asked, shutting off the car.

"He lived in a foster home." She glanced over at Amy. "They had no clue where he'd gone, but since he'd turned eighteen a month before..." She shrugged. "Since it was clear that he'd taken his belongings, they figured he'd gone it on his own."

"How terrible." Amy shook her head. "To grow up without a family."

There was something in her sister-in-law's eyes that had Laura shifting. When she watched a tear roll down her face, Laura reached for her hand.

"Hey, is everything okay?" she asked her.

"I'm sorry." Amy covered her face. "It's just... we've been trying..." She dropped off.

"Trying?" Laura asked.

"I... I think it's my fault. The doctors..." Amy shook her head and sniffled. "It's just... after Kristen became pregnant with Jade... And we still hadn't conceived." She glanced at her. "We started trying and here it is ten months later with no luck. We've talked about adoption... if..."

"Hey." Laura gripped Amy's hand. "Don't rush these things. But adoption is a wonderful choice. I know what it was like growing up around Simon. How he dreamed of finding a wonderful family of his own. Any child would be lucky to have you two as parents. If it's meant to be... It will happen."

"Thanks." Amy wiped her face and sobered. "It doesn't excuse Simon for abandoning you."

Laura could tell that Amy had cleared her mind and was once again focused on Laura's pain instead of her own.

"Did he break your heart?" Amy asked after they were seated in a tall booth in the restaurant.

"Yes," she answered truthfully. "I haven't trusted a man since," she admitted.

Amy's blonde eyebrows shot up. Laura could tell why her brother had fallen for the pretty blonde. The woman was not only beautiful outside, but inside as well. She was kind and very easy to talk to.

Laura could vaguely remember Amy from when they'd lived in Golden, before they'd moved away after their parents' divorce. Amy and Logan had gone to school with one another. To hear Amy's stories, her brother used to torment her all the time. To hear Logan's side, he'd known back then that he'd love Amy.

As they ate lunch, she told Amy everything that had happened between her and Simon. How they had turned from best friends to lovers one night after a friend's party. How they had been practically inseparable all throughout high school. They'd been the couple most likely to marry and still be together at all the school reunions.

"When Simon took off, and I was left to walk graduation all by myself, it devastated me," she said over her last bite of tacos. "I remember thinking that he'd just... return. That he'd show up for graduation and surprise me and things would go back to how they were." She closed her eyes as her heart filled with the memory of the pain she'd suffered. Still suffered. "Each day he didn't return pained me more than the one before. I turned to my career and school."

"I'm sorry." Amy shook her head. "I can't even imagine. I know that when your family moved away from Golden... I was so thankful when Logan came back into my life." Amy suddenly stopped and her smile grew.

"What?" Laura asked, concerned for her sister-in-law.

Then Amy started laughing. "I have a wonderfully sinful idea about how to pay Simon back."

Laura thought about getting the man back for all the pain he'd given her over the years and leaned forward. "I'm all ears."

$\mathcal{L}$unch with Logan Miller would have intimidated Simon years ago. He had, after all, always looked up to the man.

Now, however, sitting across from Logan was like sitting across the table from an old friend. Actually, Logan had, for the entire time Simon had been dating Laura, been like an older brother to Simon.

Considering Simon had never really known what a family could be like, his young mind had melded into the Millers as if they were his own. Looking back, he figured it was one of the reasons he'd never been adopted. He already had a family. One that he'd turned his back on the moment he'd gotten into trouble. Of course, back then it had been his only choice.

Now, he waited for their drinks to be delivered to answer Simon's question about what he'd been doing with himself over the last five years.

The question should have been, what hadn't he done?

At first, he'd run. Hid. Plotted a way back to Laura. Then, when it was made apparent that, if he returned, he would endanger the woman he loved, the family he'd adopted as his own, he'd taken off and traveled.

Using the small amount that he'd saved up for a wedding ring for Laura—he'd planned to ask her to marry him on graduation night—he'd moved around England instead. When he'd run out of money, he'd gotten a delivery job. When he moved on from England and hit the road once more, he'd gotten a different job. He stayed on the run because he knew that if he stopped, he would want to come back to the one place he couldn't afford to. He'd come back to the family he'd always wanted.

As days continued to flow into months and years, the jobs got better, and his bank account grew. He never really settled down to one field of work, but three years ago, he suddenly found himself in Chicago purchasing a small defunct strip mall. He turned the place around and purchased two properties along the South Carolina coast that had been damaged by a hurricane the year before. After turning those properties around, he made his first million.

The following year was a blur of purchasing properties and flipping them into profits. He hadn't known he'd have such a knack for it, but one day, he realized that he finally had enough power to overcome the obstacles that had kept him from happiness.

So, he'd turned his eyes back to Colorado and started his way back to Laura.

He'd never really lost track of her. Even during all his travels, he knew exactly where she was. What she was doing.

He'd come up with the idea for ReNewed Foster Care Facility back when he'd been shuffled from one foster home to another. The first thing he'd done was search for a property that would fit his needs.

Knowing that Laura was living and working in Golden had

narrowed his choices down to the area. After discovering the quaintness of the small foothill town, he'd been thankful when he'd found the old red brick building. He'd had his employee call RMR to broker the deal in hopes of running into her back then.

In the past eight months, while construction was in full swing on the building, he'd traveled around the States and had tied up all his loose ends. He'd sold off the remaining properties so he could focus on his new projects closer to home.

He'd even purchased a home in the foothills, not far from Golden, sight unseen. When Kristen had backed out of working on the interior of the building because of her new baby, he'd gently suggested working with RMR since he knew the two companies worked close together. Actually, the close relationship was why he'd chosen Urban Development in the first place.

He'd read an article a few years back on how the two companies had worked on a large project together. He'd also known about Kristen and Amy's friendship, as he'd seen them together in wedding pictures that had been posted on the social media pages for the companies.

"So?" Logan asked again. "Five years... You must have thought to come back around long before this?"

"More times than I want to admit," he replied.

"What kept you away?" Logan asked, leaning forward. "Why'd you leave in the first place?"

"That's not as easy of a question to answer as to why I'm back."

"We've got an hour. I'm all ears," Logan said, leaning back slightly and crossing his arms over his chest.

Looking at the man, Simon knew there no way around giving Logan some answers. He had hoped that Laura would hear his reasoning from him. She deserved hearing it directly from him.

"Do you remember that I grew up in foster care?" he asked.

"Yes," Logan answered. "It's one of the reasons I agreed to put Laura on the project full time with you. It's something we've both been passionate about because of growing up around you."

"A couple weeks before graduation"—Simon took a deep breath— "I turned eighteen and everything changed."

As he filled Logan in on his desperate and crazy past, the man sat silently listening. Simon could see the anger and the pain flood his eyes. How he'd tracked down his real parents and opened a portal to the hell he'd ended up running from.

"What do you need from us?" Logan asked when he was done with his story.

Simon hated concerning the man, or anyone else around the business, but he figured that someone needed a heads-up that there might be a crazed madman lurking around the corners and sending goons after him.

"I think things are under control. Finally." He sighed. "Which answers your other question of why I'm back now."

"Yeah, so, you think it's really safe?" Logan asked.

"For now." He nodded and felt the weight that had held him down for years lift slightly.

"Okay." Logan shook his head. "Laura would have understood. We all would have. You may not have known this, but when you left, you not only broke her, you broke our family. We all pretty much looked at you as ours. Even our mother was heartbroken."

Simon felt his chest tighten and reached up to rub the spot as he swallowed. "Yeah, leaving was the only way I could ensure everyone's safety."

At this point, they had both already finished their burgers and fries.

Logan was quiet for a while more and then shook his head. "We'd better head back."

"Until I have time to talk to your sister and tell her everything I just told you, I'd appreciate keeping this between us," he said as they walked out through the snow to Logan's truck.

"Sure, it's your story to tell, not mine." Logan shook his hand. "I'm sure glad you came back, and I'm excited for my sister to work on the project with you, but…" Logan pulled Simon closer and narrowed his eyes slightly. "If you break her heart like you did last time"—his hand tightened on Simon's— "I won't be so forgiving."

Simon smiled. "I always looked up to you like a big brother. I wouldn't expect anything less than a threat like that. Actually, I've been waiting for it since the moment I first contacted you about working together."

Logan laughed and released his grip. "Now that the unpleasantries are over, we'd better get back so you can get to work. I hear you're trying to get this done before Christmas?" he asked after they climbed in the truck.

"Yeah, it would answer a lot of Christmas wishes. Some of the old facilities are not up to quality standards. It's the best present I can think to give the kids." He shrugged. "Besides families of their own."

"Damn." Logan sighed. "If my sister doesn't fall for you all over again, I'll adopt you myself," he joked, causing Simon to smile.

When Simon walked back into Laura's office, he couldn't help but smile at the sight of her. Her hair was slightly damp from the fresh snow falling outside. She still had her jacket on and was busy reading something on her computer.

When she sensed him, she turned her chair around slowly and glared at him. "You neglected to mention that you're the owner of ReVision Development."

His eyebrows shot up. "I didn't keep it from you on purpose."

"Didn't you?" She crossed her arms slowly over her chest.

He removed his coat and took his time shaking the snow from it and hanging it up on the hook by the door.

"What else have you kept from me?" she asked.

He smiled. "I've only been here for three hours," he reminded her as he sat down. "Besides, you made it very clear this was a business relationship." He waited and watched as she debated and struggled with having her own words thrown back at her.

"Fine." She turned back around.

"I was thinking of heading to the job site. It would be good for you to come see everything for yourself. You know, get a vision of what I'm thinking."

She glanced over her shoulder at him. "Fine," she said and turned back around.

"I'll give you some time to look over the plans first." He motioned to the monitor where she had pulled up Urban Development's diagrams of the facility. "We can head out in about an hour?"

"Sure," she said over her shoulder at him.

"If you have any questions…" He moved to stand behind her again.

"Hm," she answered as she scanned the plans.

"Did you have a nice lunch?" he asked, deciding the change of subject would throw her off or at least shake her up slightly.

She glanced up at him and shrugged. "It was fine. How about yours?" Her eyes scanned his, and he knew instantly that she was looking to see if her brother had scolded him.

"Good. Your brother and I had plenty of time to catch up. Something I had hoped you and I could do. Say, after we head over to look at the facility?"

She turned back towards him. "That's not a good idea."

"Why not?" He smiled down at her. "Afraid?" He knew that she had always risen to a challenge. There had been only a few times he hadn't been able to get her to agree to something without challenging her first.

Once again, he watched her struggle to come to a final decision.

"Show me your facility first, then we'll talk." She turned back to the computer and continued to scan the plans.

It was the most he could hope for. A chance. He knew he didn't deserve a second chance with her, but finally, this was his chance at happiness. His chance to win her back. To show her exactly what she meant to him.

CHAPTER 5

There were so many things that Laura wanted to say to Simon. She needed him to know the pain he'd put her through. All the years she'd wasted waiting for him to return. And now he waltzed back into her life and expected to pick things up as if he'd never left.

Over lunch, she and Amy had come up with a plan to pay him back. Not that she was totally behind it, but she had remembered hearing Amy talk about how she'd paid Logan back for all the hell he'd put her through as a child. The fact that they had ended up together made her realize even more how perfect they were together.

Part of her wanted to pay Simon back, while the other part wanted to ignore him and hope that he'd go away again. Just being in the same room with him stung.

"Ready?" Simon said, breaking into her thoughts.

Since she'd been daydreaming for the past half hour, she figured it was no use stalling.

"Sure." She locked her computer and pulled her purse from the bottom drawer of her desk. When she glanced around for her coat, she realized she was still wearing it. Every time she returned from lunch, she was always chilled. She'd debated getting a small space heater for the room but hadn't had a chance to buy one yet.

Pulling on her gloves, she followed him outside and stopped in front of a new black Porsche SUV.

"It appears you've done well for yourself over the past five years," she said sarcastically as he opened the door for her.

Instead of answering, he shut her in the car and walked around to the driver's side and climbed in.

"It's a lease," he said finally.

"Not even able to commit to a car?" she teased.

"I would expect that the fact that I'm starting a long-term facility for wayward children is proof enough that I'm back to stay." He pulled out of the parking lot.

"Businesses can be run from anywhere. But you know that. I hear that ReVision was born in Chicago. Tired of the windy city?"

He smiled and glanced over at her. "You can say there was little there to hold my interest for long."

He was deliberately being charming, and it was driving her a little crazy. They had never really kept secrets from one another, but now, it was as if she didn't know who he was. Not really. Not anymore.

She couldn't lose sight of exactly whose fault that was.

"So then, you're back to stay?" she asked, trying to sound nonchalant.

"Yes. I've purchased a home in the hills." He motioned to the hills surrounding Golden.

Her eyebrows arched up. "So, you're at least able to commit to a home…" She smiled. "Don't let your car hear that. It might get jealous."

He chuckled and she realized just how much she'd missed

the sound of his laughter. It too was intoxicating, almost as much as his deep blue eyes.

She had barely been paying attention to where they were going since she knew the old Coors building that he'd purchased. She'd driven by the massive thing for years when she'd returned to town to visit their old home. However, since it was on the other side of town, she hadn't driven past it in the past few months.

Now, as they approached it, she realized that so much of the building had changed. The outside was almost completely renovated. How had no one in town been talking about this?

Surely, someone in the small town would have mentioned it before now. Then again, she'd been so busy with work that she hadn't really had a lot of time to come up for air.

"They're almost done." She motioned towards the building.

"Yeah, they'll finish the grounds next spring. It's hard to plant grass when there's a few feet of snow." He parked next to a few construction vehicles. "We'll head in the front doors. I'll tell the foreman we're here." He reached behind him and pulled out two hard hats. "Safety first," he joked.

"Right." She took the hat and climbed out of the SUV and followed him to the front of the building. Already, she could see the amazing work that had been done to transform the old storage facility into a friendlier, warmer home for children and teens.

"Tell me what your vision is," she asked as they pulled on their hard hats.

As they stepped inside, he started talking about a warm reception area with large family meet-and-greet areas just up the wide staircase on the second floor. As they passed the foreman, Simon mentioned that they would be walking through the facility and answered a few questions the man had about several issues that had come up.

They continued the tour down a long hallway, where he

showed her where the library and cafeteria would be. They walked by a massive gymnasium. "There are boys' and girls' showers in the back." He motioned. "There's even a bowling alley and an indoor swimming pool."

"What can I do around here?" she asked.

"For these common areas we're wanting warmth and comfort but sturdy furniture." They made their way towards a large arched staircase.

"This is amazing." She ran her fingers over the new wood banister.

"We had to turn the massive, gutted building into three floors of space. The main floor is for common areas. The second floor is learning and family meeting areas, and the third-floor houses all the bedrooms and private areas," he told her as they stepped onto the second-floor landing. "This floor will be more of the same as far as decorating goes. Upstairs is where I'll want to personalize things a little more." He motioned towards the next set of stairs. She followed him up. At the top of the stairs, there was a small area that led off to two separate hallways. "Just like Harry Potter, the boys' dorms are to the left, the girls' dorms are to the right." He smiled.

She chuckled. "I'd forgotten you love to read."

"The rooms will need to be decorated for a variety of ages ranging from infant to teen," he added.

She hadn't meant for her words to sneak out, but since they had, she moved off down the hallway and stepped through a set of double doors.

"Each child will have a security bracelet that will allow them into the private areas," he said.

She turned and frowned at him. "Like a tracking device?"

"No," he balked slightly. "God, no. Like key cards."

She shook her head. "Preteens and teens won't see it as such. They'll think they're being monitored."

He smiled. "I'd thought of that. They also are tied to meals, social events, and a reward program for attending classes and helping out with the younger children." He smiled. "On the main floor there is a store area where we'll sell snacks, books, and other small incentives that can be utilized as rewards."

"You've thought of everything." She looked into the first smaller space that would become some little girl's new home. A home without parents, without brothers and sisters. Her heart broke a little at that thought. Then she remembered that Simon had been raised like that. She glanced over at him and watched him closely. "You've been thinking about this for a while."

"All my life." He leaned up against the doorframe as she walked around the empty space.

She turned towards the large windows and glanced out at the beautiful snow-covered Rockies beyond. "A home with a view," she murmured, remembering something he'd told her when they'd first become friends and when she'd first found out that he didn't have a family of his own.

"What do you mean your folks won't be here for parent-teacher night?" she'd asked him.

They were standing in the hallway, looking up at the wall filled with drawings done by their class.

"I mean, I don't have folks," he said with a shrug. "I'm an orphan."

She'd felt her thirteen-year-old heart break for the dark-haired boy that she'd secretly had a crush on for the past year. They'd grown into friends, and yet she felt her heart palpitate each time he stood close to her. Each time he looked at her with those big blue eyes that were always filled with sadness.

"Where do you live then? If you don't have a home," she'd asked.

"I have a home. It's just... more like a hotel without a view." He'd shrugged and turned his eyes away from hers.

"I think it's amazing that you want to give children something you never had." She turned away from the window now to run her eyes over him. He'd silently moved behind her and stood just a few feet away from her.

"I had a family," he said in a low voice as his eyes locked with hers. "You were all the family I needed, and I squandered that when I left." His hand moved up to her arm, holding her in place.

She felt her heart kick in her chest and instantly felt her body melt at the memories of his hands on her. What he used to do to make her feel wonderful. How he would make her body respond to his.

For a brief moment, she allowed herself to lean into him as memories raced through her mind.

Her body responded to his touch, and she willed it to not respond. To not remember how wonderful it felt being touched by him, being this close to him.

"Simon," she warned and tensed at the memory of how painful it had been when he'd left without a word.

"I know I owe you more than just an explanation, and I doubt I could ever make it up to you after how much I must have hurt you." He reached up and ran his fingertips over her cheeks. She hadn't realized she was crying. She hated that little weakness and closed her eyes on the pain.

"Please, don't," she begged. All these years, all the pain. It had filled her, consumed her for years. She'd believed she'd dealt with the hurt years ago, but seeing him again, being this close to him, had it all surfacing.

"I just want a chance to make it up to you. To prove to you that I will never disappear on you again. I'm here. Right here." He cupped her face and lowered his face until his lips brushed against hers.

The light touch of his lips on hers reminded her of the first time he'd kissed her on her fifteenth birthday.

"I'll walk with you." Simon had rushed to her side after she'd spent the evening at the football game in hopes that she'd get ten minutes alone with him. Instead, she'd spent the evening in the stands listening

to Robin Carter brag about sleeping with Rodney Harrison the weekend before while Simon played ball on the field.

Just outside of the stands, he reached over and took her hand in his. He was still wearing his uniform and cleats, and they clicked on the pavement as they walked towards the parking lot where she knew Logan waited for her. Most likely her brother would be late picking her up.

"Where's your brother?" Simon asked when they reached the dark parking lot.

"He's probably late. He's always late." She shrugged and tried to act normal. But the fact was, she was so nervous, and her voice wavered.

"Good." Simon moved closer to her and reached up to run his hand slowly down her cheek. "I've wanted to kiss you." His eyes moved down to her lips as he stepped closer to her.

She rushed to run her tongue over her lips to wet them. Wanting to hold onto every memory of her first kiss, she kept her eyes open as he moved closer to her. When their lips finally touched, she felt her entire body melt against his. Her hands ran over his football pads under his uniform, wishing she could feel him instead of the hardness of the protective gear.

Suddenly, she realized she was currently running her hands over his shoulders, reaching under his jacket to explore those new muscles she'd seen earlier. Simon took the kiss deeper while he allowed her to run her hands over him.

When a loud bang sounded from somewhere down the hallway, she came to her senses and jerked away from him. She covered her mouth with her hand quickly as she shook her head.

"No, I… no." She felt tears sting her eyes. Her throat burned and her heart ached as she turned away from him. "I've seen enough," she said, rushing towards the doorway.

"Laura." Simon grabbed her arm and stopped her from leaving. "I'm sorry. Please, don't go. Let me finish showing you around."

She almost jerked her arm free but stopped herself. This was her job. She wanted this. Wanted to do this for him and the children.

Instead of answering, she nodded in agreement. He dropped his hand and stepped back to motion for her to go on.

"For what it's worth," he said as she passed him, "I really am sorry."

CHAPTER 6

Over the next few days, Simon kept things professional between them. Still, he caught himself sneaking glances at Laura whenever she wasn't looking or when his mind wandered to daydreaming of kissing her again.

During the long days, she would work on her computer quietly, planning out each room in the facility meticulously, down to the colors of the walls, curtains on the windows, and rugs on the floors. She would make phone calls to furniture suppliers and ask him questions as they arose. He had peeked at a few of her proposed color schemes and was more than impressed.

He had believed that she would start with the girls' wing, but she'd started on the boys' rooms, beginning with the younger kids' rooms then moving up to the teenagers' rooms.

Anyone under the age of four would be together in a large nursery, which she was working on at the moment.

"When I'm done with these basic color schemes, I have a few furniture warehouses we'll need to go check out. I've called a couple of them to have them keep me posted about what they have in stock for beds, bed frames, and nightstands." She glanced over her shoulder at him.

"Impressive." He nodded to the screen. "It's like you're making my visions come to life."

She chuckled. "It's not hard, just figuring out what's in stock and if it meets your budget."

"Yes, but the colors. They're bright and cheerful yet warm and friendly." He tilted his head. "I would have never thought to put teal in the nursery."

"Most facilities like this end up dull and depressing like hospitals." She glanced back at the screen. "This is a home. A place they should feel happy, comfortable in. Bright colors will stimulate imagination and good emotions. When we look for furniture for the family visiting rooms, I'm thinking of the same colors. Maybe add a touch of coral or..." She tilted her head. "Sunshine yellow."

He touched her shoulder lightly as the memory of his own dull childhood surfaced.

How many nights had he spent in the grey-walled room that he'd been assigned to? Sure, he'd filled the walls with posters or some of his drawings, but the entire home where he'd lived from age thirteen to eighteen had been dull and depressing. It was one of the reasons he'd spent so much time with Laura and her family.

He remembered the family home that their mother had made for them. How cheerful it had been, how warm he'd felt there. It was one of the best places in his memories.

How many times had he wished he could be part of her family? How many nights had he lain awake wishing to run away and sneak into her bedroom and just... be happy?

His eyes ran over the top of her head and still felt that urge. Whether she knew it or not, she was his family. Even when he'd been on the run, she'd been part of him. Always.

"I thought we'd take a break during lunch and swing by my

friend's furniture store. Tom owns Albert's. He's married to Amber, Aiden's sister."

"The movie star?" Simon asked. "I'd heard Aiden talk about them. They're expecting their first child next spring," he answered.

"They are?" Laura turned and looked up at him with surprise.

He smiled. "Oops, I guess it's a secret for now."

"No." She shook her head. "I'm just out of the loop. I haven't talked to Amber in..." She sighed. "I'm a bad friend," she admitted with a shake of her head.

"Your brother tells me you've been busy here."

"Yeah, but..." She pulled out her phone and shot off a text to Amber. "There, now I have to send one to Ashley." She glanced up at him with a smile. "Her younger sister."

He thought about all the friends he'd been out of touch with for years. How he had practically fallen off the face of the earth five years ago and now that he was back, he still hadn't contacted anyone, except her. He swallowed the knot in his throat and sat on the edge of her desk.

"It's important to you," he started.

"Hm?" She glanced up after reading a few replies from the sisters.

"Staying in touch with the ones you care about."

"Of course, it is." Something crossed her eyes and he could tell she was remembering how he'd left her for all those years.

"I guess someone like me... How I was raised, it's different. I learned early on to never really rely on anyone else." He shifted, feeling slightly uncomfortable about opening up to her like this. Sure, in the past they had talked about his life, but he'd always kept his feelings locked up. He'd believed he had to, to protect himself. Not against her, but against everyone else.

Now, he couldn't imagine what he would do if a couple of his well-kept secrets got out.

"Why do you think that?" She turned fully towards him. "You had us. We were your family. The same one you turned your back on five years ago." She narrowed her eyes. "Do you know my brother spent almost a full year looking for you? Not to mention my mother." She gasped slightly. "I haven't called her yet to tell her you're back." She groaned and picked up her phone.

He stopped her by placing a hand over hers. "No," he said. Gina Miller was a young, recently divorced mother back when he'd first stepped foot in her home. Over the years, the woman had grown into the only mother figure he'd ever known. She'd helped him rent his first tux for prom and had gotten him through the SATs and his college applications, and he'd abandoned her just like he'd left everyone else who had mattered to him. She'd deserved better. All the Millers had. "Let me. I should be the one to tell Gina that I'm back."

Laura nodded slowly. "Suit yourself." She chuckled. "You think I reacted badly..." She shook her head and turned back around.

He felt his stomach roll. "Can I have her number?"

Laura burst into laughter. "Oh no, you don't want to do this over the phone."

"I don't?"

She shook her head. "No. I'll see if she can meet me for lunch. Someplace quiet." She typed on her phone. "There, we're meeting at Tabletop Café. I've asked her to get the back booth." She smiled up at him, and he felt his heart skip a beat at her beauty.

"Think she'll forgive me?" he asked, feeling a little more relaxed.

"Depends. You should definingly stop off and get a bundle of pink roses to smooth things out."

Flowers. Why the hell hadn't he thought to get Laura any?

He should be crawling back to her doing everything he could to win her back.

"I'll…" He glanced towards the door.

"Go, I'll meet you there in… half an hour," she added after checking her watch.

He grabbed his jacket but instead of heading out to his car, he went upstairs to find Logan.

He knocked briefly on his office door, then opened it and asked, "What's your sister's favorite…" He stopped when he spotted Amy and Logan in a heated embrace. "Sorry." He moved to close the door on the couple.

"It's okay, I was just… leaving," Amy said with a smile. "I'm going to be late for my meeting." She turned to Logan. "And I'll tell your uncle it's all your fault."

Logan laughed. "He'd believe you too." He kissed her again quickly.

As Amy passed him, she narrowed her eyes slightly. "What is Laura's favorite what?"

"Hmm? Oh. Um, flower?" he asked.

Amy smiled. "Daisies." She chuckled. "Yellow ones if you can find them. Good luck."

"Thanks," Simon called after her.

"Guess I won that bet." Logan leaned on the edge of the desk with a smirk.

"Bet?"

"Sure. We all had a pool going on how long it would take you to pull out all the stops. Flowers…" He held up his hand and started ticking off items on his fingers. "Wine, dinner, jewelry, marriage."

Simon thought about his serious lack of planning and promised himself that he would come up with a complete plan to win Laura back later that evening. Right after he found the nearest florist.

"There's a florist on Main Street, where the old bakery used to be," Logan said, as if he could read Simon's mind.

"Thanks." He turned to go and glanced down at his watch. Twenty-five minutes to go.

When he stepped into the café, he realized he'd never felt more nervous than he did at that moment. Not even when he'd waited in the conference room for Laura to arrive.

Maybe it was because he knew that if Gina didn't accept him back, Laura would never let him back in completely either. Whatever the reason, he knew this was the biggest chance he had at winning Laura back.

Seeing Laura wave to him from the booth, he shifted the two bundles of flowers and made his way towards the women.

When Gina spotted him, her eyes, which matched Laura's perfectly, went wide. Even though Laura's mother was easily twenty-some years older than him, she was still as beautiful as he remembered her.

He had always wondered why their mother had never remarried. Even now, he could see that her ring finger sat bare.

"Simon?" Gina's eyes teared up immediately.

"I…" He swallowed the lump in his throat. Shit. He'd been so occupied with getting the right flowers that he hadn't planned on what to say to her.

The woman surprised him by jumping out of the booth and wrapping her arms around him, smashing the flowers between their bodies.

"My boy," Gina cried as she held onto him. "You're home."

He closed his eyes and, for the first time since returning to Colorado, he really felt like he was home.

CHAPTER 7

Over the past four days, Laura had tried to keep her anger and pain to herself. But sitting in the booth at one of her favorite cafés, watching her mother hold onto Simon and cry, all the emotions she'd been hiding since his return came to a head. Well, she hadn't been hiding the anger. That one she'd gladly shown him several times already.

Wiping her eyes quickly before either Simon or her mother could see her tears, she shifted over in the booth so Simon could sit beside her.

"You knew he was back?" Her mother turned to her as she sat back down and wiped her eyes dry.

"I did. Logan knew before me." She had no qualms about throwing her brother under the bus.

"When did you return to Colorado? Where have you been?" her mother asked Simon.

Before answering, Simon handed a bundle of flowers to each of them. Laura smiled down at the smashed daisies and buried her face in them. Smelling spring, she sighed as Simon gave his drink order to the waitress.

"For a while, I was overseas," he answered when they were alone again.

Laura glanced at him a little surprised at this news. From what she'd gotten out of him, she'd believed he'd only been in Chicago.

One great thing about her mother was she had a knack for getting answers, especially out of Simon. The man opened up more to her mother than he had in the past four days sitting in a room with her.

She listened as he talked about moving around Europe for the first year after he'd left, explaining how he'd working odd jobs before returning to the States and, thanks to running into the right man on the airplane home, purchasing a defunct business in Chicago with his savings.

"It was luck really. George had been looking to offload the old building and thought he'd found a sucker when he met me." Simon chuckled. "I ran into him a month after I sold the property for twice what I paid him for it and let him know my fortune." Simon chuckled. "The man actually offered me two more properties he couldn't get rid of. I purchased one, a strip mall, and flipped it to a church for triple what he got out of me."

"That's wonderful," Laura's mother said warmly as she nibbled on her Caesar salad. "And now? What are you doing back in Colorado?"

Simon's eyes moved to hers. "I've got a project a little closer to my heart."

She felt her heart skip at the way his eyes searched her own.

"He's building a foster care facility in the old Coors building," she blurted out.

"That's what has been going on there. I've been wondering who purchased the place. There's been a lot of work going on at the property for the past year." Her mother frowned. "You've been back for over a year and didn't stop to look us up?"

Laura saw Simon wince. "I only returned myself last week. I

purchased the place sight unseen. Well, I remembered it from when I was here before, but I've been coordinating everything from Chicago while I liquidated my assets up there."

"So, you're here to stay?" her mother asked, her eyes moving over to Laura's for a flash.

"I am," he answered easily.

The simple words from him had her heart skipping with joy. But she was still pissed at him for taking off.

"Where are you staying?" her mother asked.

"I purchased a place in the hills overlooking Golden."

Her mother's eyebrows shot up. "Where abouts?"

"Indian Paintbrush Drive." He shrugged. "The place has great bones, but it's dated." He glanced towards Laura. "Maybe I'll convince your daughter to help me update it after she's done working on the facility."

She swallowed the knot that had formed in her throat. She knew the area. Indian Paintbrush Drive was an expensive street that overlooked Golden. Homes up there usually ran in the millions, even though some had been built more than twenty years ago.

"You're doing that well for yourself?" her mother asked with a warm smile. "We're so happy for you." She reached across and patted his hand. "Aren't we?" she asked Laura.

Instead of answering, Laura nodded her head.

"If possible, I'd like to swing by the facility and take a look for myself?" her mother asked Simon.

"We're having some of the furniture your daughter has ordered delivered next week. I can give you a call and meet you there?" Simon offered.

"That would be wonderful." Her mother set down her glass and sighed. "Now that all the pleasantries are out of the way..." Her mother's eyes narrowed, and Laura knew instantly what was coming. "How about you tell us, your family, why you took off in the first place?"

Simon moved to open his mouth just as Laura's cell phone went off. Glancing at the screen and seeing her brother's information pop up, she groaned. "I have to take this." She hit answer as she stepped out of the booth and made her way towards the front door.

"Hey, what's up?" she asked.

"Sorry to bug you during lunch, but there are some issues with the McCall's furnishings. Amy will explain the details when you get there, but there's a showing in less than an hour. We need you to swing by and replace the list of items I'm sending you… now." Her phone chimed.

She glanced down at the text message and groaned as she glanced back at the booth where Simon was busy telling her mother everything she'd hoped to hear.

"Think you can handle it?" her brother asked her when she put the phone back to her ear.

"Yeah," she said and hung up quickly. She made her way back to grab her coat and explained she had to leave.

For the next half hour, she rushed from store to store finding new chairs, a couple of lamps, and several paintings, then got it all in place at the McCall's home. She finished replacing the items moments before the showing, thankfully.

It wasn't the first time she'd watched her sister-in-law work to sell a home, but it was the first time a couple made an offer on the home while she stood there.

Seeing the entire sales process was thrilling.

"Congratulations on the sale," she told Amy once the older couple had left.

"Thanks." Amy smiled and leaned back in the chair, a chair Laura had picked out for the home a week earlier. The property, a million-and-a-half-dollar home that was nestled in the foothills and had sat empty for over a year, had desperately needed her help. Not only had she ordered new paint and filled it with rental furniture, she'd had to have the place professionally cleaned before stepping foot in it. Apparently, the couple had hoarded pets and had let the place go back to the bank. Thanks to her, they were getting a fat commission from the sale.

"Thanks for coming through for us," Amy said as she glanced around the home. "You have such a knack for taking an empty space and making it into something people can envision themselves in."

"Thanks." She moved away from the view of the hills surrounding the home and turned back to Amy. "Simon asked me to help decorate his place."

Amy's eyebrows rose slightly. "And?"

"And then my brother called me to fix this mess." She glanced around. "What happened here? This stuff was delivered and set up last week. Why are there suddenly missing items?"

Amy sighed. "There was a break-in last night."

"What?" Laura glanced around the place, instantly worried.

"The police have come and gone and assured us that they would find whoever broke in."

"So, the items were taken?" She frowned, remembering the more expensive items that hadn't been replaced.

"Well, no, the items that you had to replace were destroyed. Someone went through and smashed a few things, as if they were upset or looking for something in particular."

"That doesn't make sense." She glanced around. "Doesn't this place have a security system?"

"Yes, a fancy one, at that. But apparently it was shut down somehow. The company is looking into it, but..." Amy shrugged, then leaned on the table. "So, how are things going with you and Simon? Have you thought about my idea to pay him back?" she asked with a smile.

"Things are going good and, no, I don't think that anything I could do to him would equal the pain he put me through. Besides, I just don't think I could do that to someone. It's not like I hate him..."

Amy chuckled. "I didn't hate your brother when he came back into my life either. Despised, yes, but hate?" Amy shook her head. "But there was some sweet payback when I knew that he'd gotten locked in the stairwell for a few minutes." She chuckled.

"Remind me to never piss you off," Laura joked.

"They were all harmless little things that your brother had put me through as a child." Amy shrugged.

"He was terrible before the divorce," Laura remembered.

She saw Amy sober up. "Yes. I didn't know back then everything the pair of you, really, the three of you, had lived through."

Laura shrugged. "Logan got the worst of it, really."

"Yeah." Amy sighed and stood up, and then turned sheet white. She would have hit the floor if Laura hadn't rushed forward and grabbed her and forced her to sit back down.

"I guess I shouldn't have skipped lunch," Amy said, resting her head in her hands.

"Dizzy?" she asked, sitting next to her.

"A little light-headed." Amy shook her head.

Laura smiled. "Any chance you're pregnant?"

Amy glanced up at her. "N-no." She shook her head again. "I just finished my period." She sighed. "I wish... but... no."

"Some women continue to have their periods during pregnancies," Laura said. "My mother was one of them. She told me the horror story of not knowing that she was pregnant with Simon until someone asked how far along she was. By then, she was five months pregnant."

"Really?" Amy asked as she ran a hand over her stomach. "Do you think..."

"It would be worth a trip to the drug store." Laura touched her sister-in-law's hand. "Unless you've passed out when you skipped lunch before."

Amy frowned. "Never."

Laura smiled. "Finally, maybe I can become an aunt."

"Oh god." Amy covered her mouth with her hands. "We've been trying for so long." She closed her eyes. "I can't afford to get my hopes up."

"Okay, so let's run to the store now and come back and take the test here," Laura suggested.

Amy glanced around. "I... Okay," she said suddenly. "Let's do this."

"I'll drive." Laura helped her up more slowly this time. "We'll go through the drive-through and grab you something to eat while we're out."

CHAPTER 8

Since his trip to the furniture store with Laura was canceled, he headed over to the job site after lunch to make sure everything was still going smoothly and on schedule. He sat in the car on a conference call, and then, since the weather was holding up, walked around the grounds for a while before heading inside.

Since returning to Colorado, he'd tried to be as hands-on as possible at the job site. He knew that Aiden and his team, along with the construction crew, had a handle on things. But he liked to watch the process of things coming together firsthand.

Most of the work that had needed to be done was on the inside of the building since it had only been a shell with open floors and an old elevator shaft.

Now, the majority of the work was done. The workers had started the final paint jobs for each room in the colors Laura had picked out.

They had visited the site numerous times, and he'd stood by while she'd held up a wheel of color options in each room. When he'd suggested that they paint all the walls one color, she'd glared over her shoulder at him and then laughed without addressing his statement.

From then on, he'd stayed out of her way and let her work, helping her out by writing down the information she requested.

He enjoyed watching her work and went with her every time she needed to visit the site.

Now, as he walked around the massive building, he realized the place seemed empty without her there. He spent the first hour down in the office area where he knew the staff would be set up. He'd already hired a few employees, and they had turned around and hired a few more caregivers and workers. There was a thorough vetting process to make sure anyone who would be working with the children was mentally and emotionally fit and well trained. They would be periodically evaluated by him and his head of staff, Barbara Williams.

The woman was already working for him in a small rental facility in downtown Golden. She was the one dealing directly with the Colorado State Foster Care Association to get the new facility certified.

So far, everything was running smoothly, just as long as the facility was done on time.

"All alone today?" one of the workers asked him as he glanced around, no doubt looking for Laura.

"Yes," Simon answered with a slight frown. "Is your GC around?"

The man shrugged slightly and waved in the direction of the stairs, then turned back to his work as another worker nudged him.

Simon thought about the man's eagerness to see Laura and vowed right then to make sure he always went with her to visit the job site again.

He found Joe McCaw, the general contractor, in the hallway on the third floor, overseeing the painting of each room.

He shook the man's hand, and Simon let him fill him in on

the progress. Then he asked the man to give him a call if Laura ever showed up on-site alone.

"Problems?" the man asked.

"No, just… I want to make sure our visions for the place line up," he lied easily.

"No problem, boss," the man said with a smile. "We should be out of here late next week."

"That soon?" he asked, looking around at the still-messy area surrounding them.

The man chuckled. "It may not look like it, but after the paint dries, the cleaning crew will come in. They'll need about four days to work their magic. Then we'll get the final inspection and get the CO, certificate of occupancy. At that point, your lady friend can start moving everything in here." The man glanced around as if looking for Laura.

"Laura had other commitments," he said, wondering if it had been so very obvious to everyone that Laura was more than just a work associate. Maybe it was the obvious way he looked at her that clued everyone in?

"You sure have done something wonderful here. The kids are going to love it. You know, my sister and her husband adopted last year. When they found out I was working on the place, I think they decided it was about time to add another member to their family. They're looking forward to visiting the facility once it's opened," Joe continued.

Simon smiled. "That's good news." He glanced around again and realized that most of the mess in the hallway was plastic to protect the flooring from paint splatter.

"I heard you're hoping to have this place opened before Christmas?" Joe asked. "Do you think Laura can fill it with furniture by then?"

He smiled. "If anyone can do it, Laura can."

"Thanks for the vote of confidence," Laura's sexy voice sounded from directly behind him. He turned around to see her standing in the hallway, watching them as if she'd been there a while. She'd changed out of her dress pants and sweater into a pair of old jeans and a sweatshirt. Her hair was tied up in a messy bun.

"Looks like you're ready to go to work," Joe said as he slapped Simon on the shoulder. "I'll keep you posted when we'll be out of your way." Joe nodded to Laura as he passed her by.

"You should have called me and let me know you were done," he said and instantly regretted his words when her eyebrows shot up. "I would have…" He glanced around and shook his head. "Never mind. Did you get everything replaced?"

A strange smile crossed her lips just before she turned away from him to scan the room they stood just outside of.

"Wow, they're done in here already." She stepped into a clean room.

He'd been so busy talking with Joe that he hadn't looked into any of the rooms yet. Following her inside, he realized just how close they were to finishing.

The room that would hold two young adolescent boys was completely ready for furnishings.

Laura turned back towards him. "When can I get to work in here?" she asked as she turned back towards him.

"Joe seems to think the end of next week. Which will give you two full weeks to finish all this before the date we'd like the staff and the first of the kids to move in." He glanced around again. "Think you can do it?"

She smiled. "With some help, yes."

"Good." He rubbed his hands together.

"Ready to hit the furniture stores?" she asked with a slight dip of her chin.

"Yes. Maybe we can swing by my place so I can lose the suit?"

Her smile instantly slipped slightly.

"While I'm changing, maybe you can look over the home and

For a split second, he watched heat flood into her gaze. She was assessing him as if she was trying to figure out how to swallow him whole.

His body instantly reacted to her desire. Without thinking, he closed the space between them and pulled her into his arms.

The moment their lips touched, it was like returning home. She fit against him perfectly as if they had been made for one another.

This time, she was the one who took the kiss deeper as she ran her hands over his arms and chest hidden under his sweater.

"Simon," she sighed against his skin as he ran his mouth down her neck to the exposed skin just above her sweatshirt.

"My god, I've missed you," he murmured as he trailed his fingers up under the hem of her sweatshirt to run his fingertips over her soft skin. "I've dreamed of you all these years."

"I..." She shook her head. "I can't." She nudged him backwards. He dropped his hands and took a giant step back.

Hell. He knew he'd pushed it. He'd promised himself he was going to explain everything to her and here it was, days later, and he hadn't even told her why he'd left.

"Laura," he started, but she held up her hands to stop him.

"No, don't." She sighed and shook her head. "I think we can both agree that it would be a bad idea for anything to happen between us now. We have a history and because of that history together, there are bottled up feelings." Her eyes met his. "Feelings I no longer have. Nostalgia. That's all it is. That's all it can be." She straightened her sweatshirt and brushed her hair with her fingers to put it back up in the messy bun. He must have pulled it free when he'd been kissing her.

He hadn't even realized he'd run his hands through her soft tresses. Closing his eyes, he tried to block out the memory of how wonderful she'd felt in his arms. How sweet she'd tasted and how sexy she'd smelled. Too much. She'd been too much and his senses were vibrating and demanding more.

"Now, why don't you show me the rest of your place so that while we're at the store I can be on the lookout for items to replace all this." She motioned around to the room and, before he could respond, she walked away.

Watching her back, he realized just how much it must have hurt her when he'd left all those years ago. He'd been such a fool.

CHAPTER 9

Okay, so Simon's place was a direct blast from the nineties. Which would have been okay if the decorator had had any real taste. Still, it had good bones and a killer view. The kitchen and living spaces were big and easy to modernize. The basement with its shag carpet and dated furnishings could be gutted and turned into a beautiful space.

All of the bedrooms could be easily updated as well. The bathrooms that she'd quickly gone through needed the most work. Pink and teal tile filled two bathrooms. The third was a simple powder bath that would just need fresh paint.

She stepped into the very feminine mauve-painted main bedroom and couldn't help herself from bursting out laughing.

"You're staying in here?" She turned and looked at him. He was scowling, which made her laugh even more.

"Yes. Now you can see why I want it redecorated," he said in a low tone.

If the walls hadn't been bad enough, the massive four-poster oak bed would have tipped the scales for her.

"We're going to have to get a chain saw and cut that thing apart to get it out of here," she said, walking around the bed.

He chuckled. "I'd be happy to do the honors. The thing is highly uncomfortable to get in and out of."

"Why not set up in one of the other rooms?" She smiled. "There was a teal room just down the hall."

He glared at her. "Having fun?"

She chuckled. "Okay, enough. I think I've seen everything I need to. Let's head out and see what we can find."

"Gladly." He followed her back out of the room, and when they stepped outside, big snowflakes were falling, slowly building up on the ground.

"Here it comes," she said as she took in the fresh mountain air. "They said it was supposed to get bad later tonight." She glanced at her watch and realized it was just past three. If they were lucky, they would have five hours to shop before the stores closed. That would be enough time for her to shop for a small project, but with the massive facility still needing some mattresses, a few bed frames, and furniture for the main areas, she figured she'd need at least a full week to fill every room. Not to mention starting on Simon's place.

"Why don't you leave your car here?" Simon suggested.

She turned slowly to him as she narrowed her eyes.

"You know." He smiled. "To help save the environment and all."

She thought about the drive into the city and figured that they could use the drive together to talk about what he had in mind for his home.

"Sure." She pulled her purse and the leather binder with all her notes out of her car and climbed into his SUV. She enjoyed the warm leather seats as he started heading down the mountain.

"Do you have a security system?" she asked as they passed the house she and Amy had been in earlier.

"Not yet." He glanced at her. "Why?"

"That place was broken into last night." She motioned to the house as they passed it.

"It was?" His arms jerked slightly, causing the car to jolt.

"Easy." She held onto the handle above the door.

"Sorry," he murmured. "Did the police catch who broke in?" He kept his eyes on the road.

"No." She relaxed slightly. "Amy says it was probably some local kids. They smashed some stuff up and didn't take anything." She glanced out the window and enjoyed the ride down the hillside.

He remained silent for a while until she asked him if he had any ideas about what he wanted his place to look like when it was done.

"Better," he responded. "Modern."

She smiled. "Okay, you don't have any eccentric tastes?"

He glanced at her soberly. "As far as my home style, no." His eyes ran over her and once again she felt her entire body heat. Damn. She seriously needed to get herself under control around him.

"When are you wanting your place finished?" she asked.

He shrugged. "After the facility is done. It doesn't matter as much as getting the kids into their new place for the holidays," he answered, and she felt her body warm for a completely different reason.

"Are we going to talk about it?" she finally asked after a few more moments of silence.

"Hm?" he asked as they hit the main highway.

"Why you left. Or are you just going to tell all my family members and not me?" His expression changed, and she knew that he was thinking about it.

"I'd hoped to tell you first, but your family…" He shook his head. "I wanted to tell you first."

"So, tell me now." She shifted slightly so she could watch him.

He glanced her way and sighed. "The condensed version is, I left town for everyone's safety."

"No. We have about twenty minutes until we get to Albert's Furniture. That should be plenty of time for the extended version." She crossed her arms over her chest and waited.

"I found my father," he said finally. "The day after I turned eighteen, I asked the agency for my records to be unsealed and... well, let's just say that when I showed up on his doorstep... things didn't go as I had dreamed and planned my entire life."

"You never told me." She felt her heart break slightly for what he'd gone through all on his own.

"There's a reason." He glanced at her. "My dad is Joseph Wilson."

She gasped. "The senator? The one who is suspected to be involved in..."

"Major crime syndicates? Apparently, he's been happily married for thirty years, but rumors have circulated that he's cheated on the elections to win his seat and taken bribes from the mob and foreign countries." He sighed. "When I showed up on his doorstep alive and well, ignorant to the fact that I looked just like he looked at my age, he threatened me." He shook his head. "He threatened everyone I cared about and then told me if I didn't get off his property, he'd have the legal right to shoot me dead. He said he'd claim some no-good orphan had been trying to break into his mansion."

She felt the sting as if it had been her instead of him.

"I'm so sorry." She touched his hand. "What do you mean... alive and well?" she asked once his words sunk in.

Simon sighed. "My mother, reportedly a lady of the night, had taken money from my father to have me... removed."

Her hand tightened on his. "Simon, I'm so sorry."

He shook his head. "I tried tracking her down, but, apparently, she was found in an alley with a needle in her arm a few months after I was born."

Laura closed her eyes and felt tears building up. "You have us," she said, taking his hand in hers. Then she thought about everything he'd said. "You left because he threatened us?"

"No. Shortly after I left my father's place, I met you and your brother for dinner. I spotted two muscular goons watching us. One of them had a camera and was taking pictures of you."

She felt her heart skip again. "How do you know they were sent there by your father?"

"I confronted them. They told me the senator didn't like me sticking around too close. He didn't believe I wouldn't go to the press. They handed me a ticket along with a picture of you, cut in half, and told me if I wasn't on the plane and if I ever contacted any of you or told you or anyone what was going on, I'd never see you again."

"My god." She shook her head. "That's… crazy."

He sighed. "Yeah, tell me about it."

"Stuff like this doesn't happen. Does it?"

"I wish I'd never looked into my birth parents," he said under his breath.

"You couldn't have known," she said softly.

"When I saw his name… I could have…"

"Hey, it's not your fault," she soothed him. "You obviously feel comfortable coming back here now."

He glanced at her. "Don't hate me," he warned.

Her eyes narrowed. She knew that look and tone in his voice all too well.

"What have you done?" she asked.

He motioned behind them and waited for her to spot the dark car behind them.

"Oh god! You don't think that's him, do you?" Fear spiked through her.

"God, no." He took her hand. "That's my security. I've had them watching you for a while now. I have someone watching your brother and mother as well."

She balked. "You… what?" She jerked her hand away. "Does my family know this?"

"They do now. And after I explained everything, why I left in the first place, they agreed to the extra precaution."

She felt a slight headache grow and instantly wished to talk to her family.

"How long have you had someone watching me?" she asked, feeling a slight jump in her gut. She'd never been paranoid but, for the past few months, she'd believed she'd seen the same dark sedan sitting outside her place. She'd chalked it up to someone new moving into her apartment complex, but now she wasn't so sure.

He shrugged. "Does it really matter?" he asked as he turned off the highway. When she remained silent, he sighed and answered. "A few months. I wanted to make sure that my father wouldn't try something when word got out that I was coming back to Colorado."

"Do you think he would still come after us? I mean, it's been five years." She felt her chest ache now.

"No," he said too quickly.

"Something tells me you don't believe that."

He sighed loudly. "I hope not," he corrected. "The security is an added precaution." He pulled into the parking lot of Albert's Furniture. He parked, turned off the car, and turned towards her. "If I believed any of you were still in danger, I wouldn't have come back here."

Looking into his eyes, she suddenly realized that everything she'd been through over the past five years paled in comparison to what he'd gone through. What must it have been like for him? Finding his father. Having the man threaten him, threaten them.

She felt like a selfish fool. For the past five years, she'd never once thought of what might have happened to him to send him running away from the only family he'd ever had. The only people who had ever loved him.

For the first time since he'd returned, she looked into his eyes and realized that leaving had cost him everything.

CHAPTER 10

Simon could tell that Laura was struggling with something. She kept looking at him as they walked through the massive furniture store. When she wasn't writing notes in her notebook, she was deep in thought.

"So?" he said as they walked out after purchasing several major items from her list. "I never thought I'd be cutting a check for so much just on mattresses," he joked.

She stopped walking and turned to him. "We actually got a great deal…"

"Hey." He touched her arm. "I was joking." He shook his head as his hands ran up and down her coat. "How about we take a break and grab some dinner? We should still have enough time to hit the other stores after."

She glanced down at her watch and took in a deep breath. He saw a puff of air as she exhaled. It had been snowing off and on since they'd left his place. Now the snow had stopped, leaving a light dusting all over the ground.

"Sure, there's a place not far from here." She pulled her coat tighter and shivered.

"Come on." He took her hand and rushed to the car. "I'd

forgotten how quickly the temperature can drop when the sun goes behind the mountains." They got in the car, and he cranked the heater.

"It always felt colder in Illinois," she said with a shrug.

"How many times have you been up there?" he asked as he pulled out of the parking lot.

"A few." She glanced at him. "Did you ever come back here before now?"

"No, the Friday before I came into the office was the first time I'd been back to Colorado since... the day my father's goons bought the plane ticket for me."

"You could have called," she said, and he could hear the hurt in her voice. "Told us what was happening?"

He shook his head. "I couldn't. The senator has too long of a reach. Besides, I didn't have a cell phone back then, remember?"

"Right." She sighed. "Simon, part of me wants to be upset at you still. The part that, deep down, is still hurt that you'd be able to walk away so easily."

"Believe me," he interjected as he glanced over at her, "nothing about walking away from you was easy."

She nodded slowly. "Okay."

He pulled into the parking lot of the restaurant she'd suggested and turned off the engine again.

Reaching over, he took her hand in his. She was still chilled, and he rubbed her hands between his. "You were my everything. Do you know what it was like thinking..."—he shook his head quickly— "no, *believing* that you could be taken away? I would have done anything to keep you safe. Anything."

He hadn't meant to make her cry. When she used her free hand to wipe her eyes, he felt his chest tighten.

"Laura, I didn't say these things to win you back, even though I'd be happy if it helped." He figured since he was on a roll, he'd continue. "I said them because for the past five years,

I've been just as miserable as you. Maybe even more so, since I left my family, left my heart here."

She jerked her hand free from his and wrapped her arms around his neck to hold him close.

"I'm so sorry." She cried into his shoulder. "I never thought…"

He enjoyed the feeling of her in his arms again and closed his eyes to hold onto that memory. He never wanted to let her go. Then he heard her stomach growl and laughed.

"Guess we'd better head in and grab some food." He released her and jumped out to open her door for her.

"Simon." She stopped him by touching his arm lightly. "I'm really glad you're back."

They walked hand in hand into the restaurant and sat at a table by the large fireplace in the center of the room and ate dinner. He ordered steak since he knew it was one of the best places in Denver for the meal, and she ordered a chicken salad. It seemed like a waste to him, but still, he had to admit, it looked good too.

Thankfully, the conversation steered away from his disappearance five years ago to the project. She even pulled out her binder and took down a few notes.

"The question is, how many children do you expect to move in before Christmas?" she asked him after they were done eating.

He pulled out his phone and read the last email from Barbara.

"Around twenty until after the New Year. We will be booked solid by the end of January after one of the facilities in Englewood closes its doors for good."

"Wow, I guess it was lucky you came along and built this place when you did. What would have happened to those kids if you hadn't?"

"Most likely, they'd be moved to Durango or out of state." He felt a twist in his stomach as he remembered the time when he'd been fifteen when he'd almost been moved across the state. Just the thought of not being near Laura and her family had caused him to start plotting to run away and live on the streets.

How many other kids had gone through something like him? How many were now living on the streets because of a bad situation?

"You're deep in thought." Laura broke into his thoughts.

"I was just remembering the time that you convinced me not to run away," he admitted.

She smiled brightly, but still, he doubted she knew just how close he'd come to leaving for good.

"You were going to live in my brother's car." She shook her head.

"It was better than the alternative." He saw her smile slip.

"I always thought that you'd adopt a ton of kids once you were out on your own." She leaned her elbows on the table and rested her chin on her fists.

"I still plan on doing so, but after I ensure the safety and well-being of as many kids as I can." He reached across the table and took her hand in his. "And after I have my family back."

Her hand jerked slightly at his touch.

"Simon, I'm… it's true that I'm happy you're back, but I don't think it would be wise if we…" She dropped his hand and waved between them. "This…" She shook her head. "I just don't think…" She dropped off as if searching for the right words.

"Laura, I'm prepared to wait forever if I need to. I know that I've hurt you and even though you now know the reason that I had to leave… I understand that doesn't fully release me from all wrongdoing. But I hope that someday we will be able to put it behind us."

Without saying anything, she nodded, and he felt his heart jump slightly at the possibility of moving forward. He hadn't expected to jump right back to where they'd left off. Hoped, yes, but expected, no. Still, knowing that she now understood why he'd left made him feel more at ease than he had before.

She hadn't turned him away or, worse, turned against him like his father had claimed her family would do once they found out about him. Found out about who his mother had been.

It was strange, but over the past five years, it hadn't bothered him that his mother had been a prostitute. Not as much as it had bothered him who his father was. What kind of man he came from.

He remembered hating the man even before he'd found out he was his father. Joseph Wilson had pushed through a state law that banned young foster kids from seeking their independence until their eighteenth birthday. Even if they could prove they could support themselves, they had to remain in the system or suffer legal consequences.

Simon had been working a full-time job at nights since the age of sixteen while attending school during the day, and he'd made enough money that he'd hoped to get a place of his own before his eighteenth birthday.

Not only had that law kept him in a foster system that no longer served him, it had also instituted a new rule that had required him to have a curfew. He'd had to be back at the facility no later than ten o'clock at night, so he'd had to cut back his hours at work, which held him back even more. If he wasn't back in his room by then, they were required to call the police and charge him. If that happened, a caseworker would be called in and he could have a criminal record. To add to it, if he showed up to school tardy, a truancy agent would visit him at the home and had the right to enforce stricter rules or even require that he stop working all together.

Every child in the foster care system was being treated as if they were criminals instead of kids with potential.

As an adult, it was one of the first laws that he had hoped to help overturn. If the kids could prove they could support themselves after sixteen, there was no reason they couldn't be on their own, with, of course, some supervision and counseling. He understood that there were some good laws in place to help foster kids from age eighteen to twenty-one. If he'd been in the States, he would have cashed in on a few of those offers himself.

"Now you're the one deep in thought," she said as they left the restaurant.

He glanced over at her and once again reached for her hand. It was something he had done without even thinking about it all those years they were together. Whenever they walked side by side, her hand was in his. Now, he frowned down at her cold fingers.

"Where are your gloves?" he asked her.

She shrugged and smiled. "I guess I left them in my car. I didn't expect it to get this cold."

He pulled his leather gloves from his jacket pocket and handed them to her.

"Thanks," she said, slipping the too-large gloves on. He smiled and took her gloved hands up and then laughed.

"I remember when we wore the same glove size," he said with a chuckle.

She narrowed her eyes. "You've grown so much since the last time I saw you. I think you're almost a foot taller."

He pulled her closer and held onto her as they stood by his car. "No, you're just getting shorter."

She laughed. "Right." She rolled her eyes.

His gaze ran over her face, taking in the blue of her eyes, the soft pink color of her checks. Her perfect smile.

"You've changed too," he said softly as he reached up and brushed a strand of her blonde hair away from her face. "Your hair is longer."

"So is yours."

He thought about it and nodded. "Yeah, the foster home used to make me wear it short."

She frowned. "They did?"

He shrugged. "It was just hair."

She lifted her gloved hands and ran her fingers through his longer locks.

"Doesn't it get in your eyes?"

"Usually, I pull it back," he admitted.

Her fingers stilled in his hair as he shifted closer to her.

"Laura, I've missed kissing you."

He heard her breath hitch and knew the moment she thought about kissing him. Her eyes moved down to his lips, and desire flooded them.

Pressing her body between his and the car, he covered her soft lips with his own until he heard her moan with pleasure.

When her gloved fingers dug into his shoulders, he wished more than anything that they weren't standing in the middle of a parking lot at one of the busiest restaurants in Denver.

When she angled and pressed her body tighter against his, he knew that if he didn't pull back now, he wouldn't be able to control himself much longer.

"We'd better…" he said, clearing his throat.

Instead of answering, she quickly nodded and jerked the car handle, only to come up short because he hadn't unlocked it yet.

"Sorry." He reached into his pocket and unlocked the car, then opened the door for her.

He slid in behind the wheel and turned to her. "Where to now?" he asked.

She ran her eyes over him and, after biting her bottom lip for a moment, answered.

"How about we head back to your place?" she said softly.

CHAPTER 11

Screw it. She was going to throw caution to the wind. Why the hell not? This was Simon after all. The only man she'd ever loved. The only man she'd ever been with.

How long had she waited? Five years. Sure, she'd dated other men but none for long and certainly none she'd ever let into her bed. It wouldn't have been fair. Not when she knew she'd be dreaming of Simon while with them.

She'd hoped that one day she'd be over Simon finally so that she could move on with her love life, but the fact was that she wasn't. And now he was back in her life. Back with excuses for breaking her heart that cut deeper than anything her imagination had made up over the years.

The fact was, she wanted him. She'd always wanted him. She would always want him. So why fight it anymore?

When she'd been sitting in the middle of the restaurant, looking across the table at him, she'd had a moment of strength. Of courage. She'd tried to convince herself that she was better off pushing him away.

But, in his arms, with those strong muscles wrapped around her body, she'd turned to putty. Just like she had always done.

Her legs had gone weak, her body had vibrated from his touch, and her mind had turned to mush.

He'd actually given her his gloves just because he didn't want her hands to be cold. She looked down at the leather gloves warming her fingers and smiled.

It had been pure hell sitting with him all week long in her office. She'd known that he'd watched her. Every time he'd moved, shifted, or breathed, she'd imagined how he would feel next to her.

Her mind had played over each and every time they'd been together in the past.

His hand reached across the car seat and took her hand in his. Then he smiled and nudged off the glove so that they were skin to skin, linking their fingers together.

"You've warmed up," he said softly.

She wanted to reply that he had no idea how warm she was now but bit her bottom lip and nodded instead.

God. Could the car go any faster? Why had they gone to the new furniture store in Aurora instead of the older store closer to Golden?

She closed her eyes and tried to keep her body from exploding as he ran his thumb across her knuckles.

"Laura?" he said softly, causing her eyes to jerk open. "Are you okay?"

Again, instead of answering, she nodded.

"We can make it, you know." He squeezed her hand.

She thought about finding some hotel for them to stay in along the drive and then realized that she'd waited five years, what was a few more moments?

"I know," she finally answered.

He chuckled. "I meant... We can recover from our past. We can win the battle brought on by my father."

She was silent as she allowed her mind to switch gears away from sex to more practical things. Like the fact that there could be a man out there who hired hitmen to hurt them.

"Right." She nodded in agreement. "We'll need to come up with a game plan." She squeezed his hand as he turned off the highway and hit the hilly road leading up towards his house.

"Simon, let's not let the man ruin one more moment of ours." She shook the dark thoughts out of her mind. There was so much she wanted to say to the man who had ruined their lives, but since he wasn't there, she wanted to enjoy her time with Simon.

He lifted their joined hands to brush his lips over her knuckles. "Agreed. For tonight"—he glanced over at her— "it's just us."

He parked next to her car and turned off the engine. She laughed when he removed her seat belt and pulled her across the center console into his lap. The laughter died in her throat as he took her mouth and kissed her.

As far as lovers went, Simon had been everything to her. She'd never experienced another man in bed, but she'd fooled around a lot over the years he'd been gone, which had confirmed that no one had ever made her feel as much as he did.

No one could come close to how Simon made her feel. It was as if her soul and his were connected. The depth to which his simple kiss could affect her was intoxicating.

"Simon, take me inside," she pleaded softly against his warm skin.

Then she was laughing again as he jerked the car door open and almost spilled her onto the snow-covered ground.

"Sorry," he groaned. He shifted her and climbed out still holding onto her.

"I can walk," she suggested as he nudged his car door shut.

"I know, but I don't want to let go of you for fear you'll change your mind." He smiled down at her.

"I won't." She wrapped her arms around his neck and held onto him.

The moment he stepped into the house, he slid her body down his and continued the kiss. She'd waited so long for this moment that she doubted she would be able to go slow.

Her fingers shook as she pushed off his coat then started working on pulling his sweater over his head. She wanted—no, needed—to see him. To feel his skin under her fingertips. To remember just how wonderful her body felt against his. She wanted all of him.

"Simon," she moaned when he wrapped his fingers around her wrists and stopped her from pulling his jeans down his hips.

"Please, Laura, I need… time. I've waited forever for this moment, and I want it to last." He nibbled on her earlobe, a move that used to drive her nuts and still did.

Her own coat and sweatshirt had landed on the floor next to his. Now they both stood in his living room in nothing but their shoes and jeans.

Simon pulled back slightly and ran his eyes over her then smiled at the silky red bra she wore.

"I like this." He ran a finger over the strap slowly. "Makes me want to discover what else you have hidden under your clothes." His fingers trailed from the strap down her ribs, over her flat belly, and played with the top of her jeans. "Laura, look at me."

Her eyes slid open and met his. She couldn't stop the low moan that escaped her lips when he opened her jeans and slid them slowly down her hips.

"My god," he sighed as he ran his eyes over the rest of her. "You're even more beautiful than I remember."

He helped her step out of her boots, then removed the jeans completely from her legs.

Standing in his living room in her matching bra and panty set made her feel empowered and bold. With her eyes locked on his, she reached for his jeans and repeated his actions on him.

Well, she tried to at any rate. His boots were a little harder to untie, and he had to sit on the edge of the sofa to help her remove them.

"Let's go into the bedroom," he said, taking her hand in his. She followed him into the mauve room and held in a chuckle at the decor.

"I know," he sighed. "Here." He turned the lights down low. "Now it's not so bad."

She walked into his arms and leaned up to kiss him. "It doesn't matter." She sighed against his mouth. "I wouldn't care where we were. Just as long as you're back with me."

He kissed her as she ran her hands over his warm skin, enjoying the strong muscles he'd gained since the last time she'd seen him.

It wasn't as if he'd been flabby before. On the contrary. He'd been a skinny kid. Too skinny. Now, however, his chest was wide, full of toned lean cords. His arms were easily double what they had been the last time they'd been wrapped around her naked body.

"You've changed so much," she said, trailing her fingers around his chest, enjoying the way his muscles flexed under her fingertips. "You started working out," she said with a smile.

His smile grew. "I did." His smile slipped. "I plan on protecting everything and everyone that's important to me by any means."

She felt his arms flex around her as her heart skipped a beat.

"Laura, I know you must..." he started, but she stopped him by placing a finger over his lips.

"Later," she said, and bumped her body against his as she laid her lips on his skin. "For now"—she ran her mouth over his taut skin— "I want to enjoy this. Enjoy you."

A loan groan emanated from deep in his chest. She marveled at how it caused his body to vibrate.

When his hands circled her waist and he hoisted her up, she

wrapped her legs around his hips and held onto him as he walked towards the bed.

"There hasn't been anyone else," he said as he gently laid her down on the bed. "Just so you know." He looked deep into her eyes.

"Only you," she agreed. She pulled his head back down to her as her fingers ran through his hair.

Making love to Simon was the same and yet different than it had been before. He was the same boy, the same man inside that he'd been all those years ago. But now there was a shadow of mystery surrounding him.

She couldn't wait to unveil it and discover what was underneath. Just as she was enjoying discovering every new cord of muscle he had, she looked forward to discovering new aspects of his personality.

He moved over her, and she couldn't help the memories from mixing in with what was happening now. Still, he would kiss her or say something new and exciting, and she'd remember that this was the new Simon, which would send waves of excitement racing through her.

She discovered a new darker trail of hair leading from the bottom of his belly button down to below his boxer briefs. She smiled and traced the line, then groaned with excitement when she nudged the material off and his dick sprang free.

He'd grown in more ways. Her body grew heated at the memory of how he'd felt the last time he'd embedded himself in her.

"Simon." She ran her fingertip over him and watched as passion flooded his eyes.

"I..." He shook his head. "Laura, I don't think I can wait much longer."

She smiled and licked her lips slowly, dreaming of how he would feel inside her now. "Don't then," she encouraged him.

In one quick motion, he changed their positions and pinned

her underneath him, holding her down with those powerful arms. His eyes met hers once more and he settled between her legs.

"I..." he started but then she wrapped her legs around his hips and pulled him to her.

When he filled her, she arched and cried out his name in pure delight. Her nails scraped his skin, trying to hold him closer to her heart.

She hadn't realized tears had leaked from her eyes until he gently brushed them away with his fingertips.

"I've hurt you?" he asked with a frown.

"No," she assured him, holding him tight. "You've healed me," she said against his lips. Then she encouraged him to move with her and forgot all of the pain he'd caused her over the past few years and focused only on the wonderful feeling of being with the man she loved again.

CHAPTER 12

There was no way Simon was going to move from the spot. He was holding Laura against his chest, cradling her in his arms as her light breathing assured him that she was fast asleep.

Glancing at the dark windows, he could see the white flakes still falling outside.

"I should head home," she surprised him by saying.

His arms tightened around her, not wanting to let her go just yet, or ever.

"Stay," he said into her hair. He placed a kiss on her head. "Please."

She sighed and relaxed further into him, laying her head on his chest.

"I'm too tired to move anyway," she said with a yawn.

"Stay the entire weekend with me," he said as he closed his eyes and held his breath, waiting for her answer.

"Simon, I…"

"What? Have work?"

"N-no. It's just…" She was silent for a while.

"We can hit your place in the morning if you need a change

of clothes and whatever." He thought about it and added. "I was hoping you'd pick out a color for this room and help me paint it?"

She sat up slightly and narrowed her eyes at him. "Trying to bribe me?"

He smiled and ran his fingers through her hair. "Is it working?"

She chuckled and sighed loudly. "Yes." She leaned up and kissed him. "I'll stay."

His hands continued to roam over her, and he felt his body growing hard against her. Her smile grew, and she leaned up and straddled his hips.

"Now," she said, placing her hands wide across his chest, "what could we possibly fill our time with?"

He leaned up quickly and took her mouth and enjoyed how she melted against him.

She tasted the same as she had all those years ago. He'd missed the feeling of her, her soft subtle scent, and the way her soft lips fit perfectly against his.

"I'll always want you," he promised her as he tucked her body underneath his again. "Always." He trailed his mouth down until he could suck her nipple into his mouth.

She'd mentioned how he'd grown in size and muscle mass. Well, she'd grown too; her breasts filled his hands now. He could spend a lifetime re-exploring every curve of hers. He'd been in such a hurry earlier that he hadn't felt like he'd really gotten to enjoy all of her. Now, however, he felt more in control and knew they had all night to enjoy one another.

No matter how she tried to hurry him along, he would pull back, slow down, and spend as much time teasing her as he could. He enjoyed watching her cheeks turn a slight shade of pink when he ran his tongue over her skin or slid a finger into her.

When he trailed his mouth lower to join his finger, she cried out and gripped his hair.

He remembered the first time he kissed her. The first time they made love. Tonight, it felt like the first all over again. He'd been just as nervous, just as anxious, and just as excited.

She had been his everything back then and now she was again. Running his hands over her body, feeling her glide her fingertips over him, he knew that he didn't want to go another day without her. Without telling her exactly how he felt.

All the things he'd kept inside of him for all those years. There was nothing he wouldn't do to win her back completely. To ensure that he had the chance to make up the missed time to her.

"Simon, please," she begged, breaking into his thoughts. When her nails dug into his shoulders, he willingly went down to her, covered her, filled her completely.

"I love you," he said against her lips. "I've loved you forever," he whispered.

For a moment, he felt her tense. Then he moved his hips, and she relaxed and wrapped her legs around him to hold on while he pleased them both.

Her hips were a little fuller than before, and he enjoyed the softness of her against him as he held onto her. She had always made these sexy little sounds when she'd come for him and didn't disappoint him this time. He felt her body tense with her release, and his wasn't far behind.

Spent. He lay there with her in his arms until their breathing calmed and he felt himself drifting off.

"I love you too," she said softly.

He smiled and pulled her closer and fell asleep with her scent filling his senses.

When he woke, it was to a chill in the air. He'd forgotten to turn up the thermostat when he'd returned home.

He grabbed the extra blanket from the foot of the bed and pulled it up over them.

"Sorry," he told her when he felt her shiver and wrap her cold legs around his. "I forgot to turn up the heat last night."

"It's freezing in here," she said between clenched teeth.

"I could get up and start a fire?"

"No, don't leave me again. You're so warm." She laid her head against his chest.

He glanced towards the windows and could see the greyness of more snow falling outside.

"It's still snowing." He ran his hands over her.

"Hmm…"

He smiled. "Still not a morning person?"

She groaned in response.

"How about I go start a fire, turn up the heat, and then cook us some breakfast?" he suggested.

Her arms tightened around him. "Instead, why don't we lay here for another hour and then you can go do all that?"

He chuckled and quickly rolled away from her.

She squealed at the chill and jerked the blankets up around her.

"You'll be warm in a few moments," he promised as he pulled on a pair of old sweats and a sweatshirt and then bent in front of the fireplace in his room to start a fire.

She mumbled something from under the blankets, but he figured it was probably better he hadn't heard the words. Her meaning was very clear from the tone of her voice. He chuckled again as he worked.

Once he was done there, he walked into the living room, turned up the thermostat by a few degrees, and started a fire in the living room fireplace as well.

Then he busied himself by making waffles, eggs, bacon, and fresh orange juice all while listening to the news on the television set that hung over the fireplace.

"What's all this?"

He turned when he'd set the last plate on the table to see her standing in the doorway, wearing a pair of his sweats and her sweatshirt. His eyes moved down to her feet and he smiled. She had found a pair of his wool socks. She still had a blanket wrapped around her shoulders.

"Breakfast." He moved over and nudged her into a chair. "Still like your coffee black?"

"No." She glanced up at him. "If you have vanilla creamer…"

His eyebrows shot up, then he nodded. "I do." He smiled. "So," he said after setting the creamer down in front of her. "What else has changed about you over the past five years?"

She glanced around the full table. "For starters, I hardly eat anything for breakfast anymore."

He shook his head. "Too bad. I guess that means there'll be more for me." He dug in.

She added some fruit to her plate and then cut a waffle in half.

"Whipped cream?" He offered her the bowl.

"Is that… Did you make that?" she asked with a frown.

"No." He chuckled. "But I did whip it a little longer and add some cinnamon."

She took a spoonful and added it with the berries onto her waffle.

He waited and watched her take a bite. She closed her eyes on a moan.

"Wow, this is amazing," she said.

"Yeah, I learned how to do that in France. Of course, I put it on crepes instead." He shrugged. "But what are waffles but thick crepes?"

She smiled at him. "You've changed a lot as well."

"Do you still like watching horror movies with the lights on?" he asked after taking a bite.

"What other way is there to watch scary movies?" she said

with a shrug between bites. "What about you? Are you still really into hockey?"

He laughed. "Yes. Even when I was in Europe, I made a point to never miss a game. I would often piss off everyone in a pub by requesting they play the hockey game instead of football."

She smiled. "I still watch the games…" She quickly glanced away with a shake of her head.

"You do?" He narrowed his eyes. "The Avalanche are doing pretty well this season."

"Seriously." Her smile grew. "Did you see…" She dropped off again.

"Why do you keep doing that?" he asked after setting down his coffee.

She shook her head. "Logan… he kept making fun of me for allowing you to corrupt me away from football."

Simon laughed. "Remind me to have a talk with your brother."

She turned her eyes towards the large windows that overlooked the hillside. He could tell she was struggling with something this morning.

"What's going on?" He reached across the table and took her hand in his.

She shook her head. "I didn't expect… for things to be this way so quickly." She turned back to him. "I was supposed to be mad at you for a while."

He smiled. "Sorry if I screwed up your timeline."

She smiled slightly. "I'm glad you did. I just don't want to take anything for granted. I don't want to skip over anything. When we were younger, everyone around us assumed…" She dropped off.

"That we would get married?" he offered.

"Yes." She nodded and frowned slightly.

"I had saved up for a ring," he admitted.

Her eyebrows jumped up. "You did?" Her frown grew.

"I was going to ask you the night of graduation." He looked down at their joined hands. "I told myself that if I came back into town and found out that you were happily married with a half dozen kids, that I would be able to move on." His eyes moved back to hers. "But I knew it was a lie."

He heard her breath hitch as her eyes filled with tears.

"Laura, you're the only woman I've ever loved. The only woman I see myself being with in the future. Screw timelines. Screw rational thought. What we have goes beyond all that."

She chuckled and wiped the tears from her cheeks.

"I'm not going to ask you now," he said easily as he looked around. "It's not the right time. But I want you to understand that that is where this is heading. That's where this has always been heading."

"Yes." She nodded. "You're the only man I've ever wanted to grow old with."

He felt his heart jump in his chest.

"Good, now that that is settled." He picked up his coffee mug. "Let's finish eating then head into the paint store and get started on covering up the pink walls in our bedroom."

She laughed. "They're mauve and…" Her smile grew. "I never agreed I'd move in here with you."

"You didn't?" He picked up a forkful of waffle. "Yet," he added before shoveling the food into his mouth.

Laura's laughter was the best sound he'd heard in years.

CHAPTER 13

*L*aura had never had as much fun painting a room as she had covering the mauve walls with Simon by her side.

Simon pulled the massive, outdated furniture away from the walls while she removed the curtains and blinds from the large windows.

"This view is so great." She stopped and appreciated the snow-covered mountains. "There isn't even another house in sight."

"Yeah, it's what I liked the most about this place." He stopped working and moved over to stand next to her. "I guess since all the windows are tinted from the outside, I don't need to hang those back up once you've taken them down." He motioned to the pile of curtains.

She glanced over at him, a little shocked.

"Of course, you need curtains." She shook her head. "The bedroom windows face east."

"So?" He turned slightly towards her.

"So!" She laughed so hard she had to hold onto her sides. He waited patiently until she stopped. "I know you're a morning person, but remember, in the summer months, the sun will be streaming in those large windows pretty early."

"Then I'll wake up earlier," he said with a shrug, but she noticed the side of his mouth twitch.

"You're messing with me." She shoved him playfully on the shoulder.

"Whatever you do, just don't hang those pink things up again." He bent down and picked up the pile of material. "I'm going to haul these out to the trash now."

"We can head to the store later to pick up some other ones. Something that goes with the color we picked for the walls." She got back to work.

After she removed all the window coverings, she taped off the baseboards, and Simon helped her tape off the crown molding by using an old ladder he had in the garage.

"So, the people that lived here before just left all this?" She walked through the filled garage.

"Yeah, when the man's wife died, the husband left everything behind and bought a yacht and is sailing around the world," Simon answered with a shrug. "They had a difficult time going through and making sure there wasn't anything personal left over." He motioned around the mess in the garage.

"You know, you could probably have an estate sale and get rid of a lot of this junk." She glanced around and spotted a few nicer pieces of furniture stored in the garage. "There's better items in here than there are in the house."

"When we're done painting, maybe we can swap out some of the pieces," he suggested.

"Great idea." She helped him move the ladder. "Just don't expect me to help lift that massive bed."

By the time they started painting the main bedroom wall, she could already imagine the finished project. The steel blue color she'd talked him into going with in the room would modernize the space. They finished the first coat and took a break for lunch. She was happily surprised when he made them a fresh chicken salad and turkey sandwiches.

After the massive breakfast, she doubted she could eat much. Still, she was hungrier than she'd thought and finished both the sandwich and the salad completely.

"Maybe after the bedroom, we can start in this room next?" he suggested as she helped him clear the dishes from the table.

"Once the furniture starts arriving next week, I have a feeling we're going to be busy getting the facility ready. That is if you're going to be open by Christmas."

"This place can wait until after." He stopped her and pulled her into his arms. "I'm just thankful you agreed to spend this weekend with me."

She smiled. "You're just thankful you no longer have a mauve bedroom."

"That too," he agreed, and kissed her.

She felt her toes curl at the simple touch. Then he pulled back and shook his head. "Come on. If we don't get in there and finish painting, I'm going to find a way to uncover the bed and take you again."

She smiled. "There are four other bedrooms in this house."

He kissed her again. "Later," he promised. "After we've had a shower. We're covered in paint."

She glanced down at the old pair of jeans and the old T-shirt she'd changed into. They had stopped quickly by her apartment to grab an overnight bag, and she'd made sure to grab clothes to paint in.

"Fine," she agreed. "Paint now, shower, then sex."

"Then dinner," he added as they stepped into the bedroom. "Wow, it's already looking a million times better in here."

She ran her eyes over the space and nodded in agreement. "I'm thinking white curtains." She tilted her head as she imagined the space. "You have such great hardwood floors throughout the house, but what you need are some area rugs.

Something that will bring in a lighter shade of blues and browns. There was a nice chest of drawers in the garage. Hopefully, it's in good shape. If not, it can be repaired, sanded, and stained. If we're lucky, there are matching nightstands to go with it." She turned slightly. "There's room for a writing desk." She motioned to a spot between the windows. "Or a small sofa." She turned to him and realized he was watching her. "What?"

He shook his head and smiled at her. "You are amazing. You can take this… mess and see something else."

She shrugged, feeling silly, and turned away from him. "It's just stuff. You move it around until it looks good."

He walked over and laid his hands on her shoulders, then turned her back towards him. "Don't knock it." He lifted her chin slightly with a finger. "I can tell you love your job."

"I do."

"But I can also tell you're unhappy working for your brother."

She sighed. "I am."

"What do you want to be doing instead?"

"This." She motioned around him, her heart racing suddenly. "Full time. I want to step foot into a place and make it a home for someone. I want to transform the old and hideous into something sleek and sexy."

His smile grew. "Then do it."

She felt her heart sink. She shook her head. "I… can't."

"Can't or won't?"

She thought about it and shrugged. "My brother—"

"Can hire someone else."

"Yes, but…" She thought about all the reasons she'd been holding back over the past year. "I don't have the money saved up to start my own business."

"I can help with that," he offered.

She straightened her back. "I don't need a handout."

He frowned. "That's not what I'm offering."

"What exactly are you offering?"

"I'm not sure. But I believe in you and want you to have everything you want." He ran his hands up and down her arms. "If you're willing to take my help, it's there," he said softly.

"Thanks," she said after a moment. "Now..." She bent down and picked up the paint roller. "Let's get this second coat done. If we hurry, we can head into town and find some curtains to hang up after it dries."

Since they finished the second coat in half the time it took to paint the first coat, they spent some time rummaging through the garage to find the chest of drawers and its matching nightstands. They even found two blue glass lamps with white shades that were a far cry better than the gaudy gold lamps.

She found a few area rugs and was excited until they unrolled them. They were worse than the ones they'd removed from the bedroom in the first place.

"Maybe while we're out getting curtains, we can look at rugs," she suggested.

"Let's move all this into the house, then we can head into town and grab some dinner while we're at it."

She glanced at her watch and laughed. "We just ate two hours ago."

He shrugged. "I've worked up an appetite."

"Okay, shopping first, then we'll find someplace to eat." She glanced down at their paint-covered clothes. "Someplace we won't be kicked out of."

She helped him move the nightstands into the house and stood back as he rolled the chest of drawers in on a small handcart. She was surprised that he was able to remove the other nightstands by himself and while he was doing that, she crawled under the bed to see if she could remove the massive headboard and footboard from the bed frame.

"What are you doing down there?" Simon asked when he returned to the room.

"We can remove the headboard and footboard." She stuck her head out from under the bed. "That will leave the bedframe, so you don't have this massive thing taking up so much space."

He knelt down and looked at the connections. "I'll go grab a screwdriver. Better yet, I saw a drill in the garage. You can do the unscrewing while I hold and remove the heavy pieces."

They worked together and, less than half an hour later, the room was cleared of all the clutter and bulky furniture. She surprised him by requesting the bed be moved from the wall where it had been to set it directly facing the wall of windows. They set the nightstands with the lamps on either side while the chest of drawers sat where the bed had been earlier.

"There." She dusted her hands off and smiled at the progress. "Once we hang the wood blinds back up and get some flowing white curtains in here, this room is going to look amazing. Too bad you don't have a large piece of artwork to hang over the bed."

"There are a few pieces in the basement we can possibly move around," he suggested. "Later. For now, let's head into town. The snow looks like it's getting worse, and I don't want to have issues getting back up the mountain after we grab some dinner."

She laughed. "Admit it, you're just hungry."

He chuckled. "Fine, I'm starved."

"Okay, food first, then we'll shop." She reached up on her toes and kissed him.

Once again, she sat back in his car while he drove down the mountain. He hadn't been lying; the snow was falling faster now. She'd lived her entire life in Colorado and could tell when a snowstorm was going to end up bad. She figured they had a couple of hours before the roads would be impassable.

Pulling out her phone, she checked the weather report and laughed when it showed the temperatures in the high seventies by tomorrow.

"What's so funny?" he asked.

"Colorado weather." She tucked her phone back into her purse. "Below freezing with eight inches of snow tonight, and seventy degrees by noon tomorrow."

He smiled over at her, and she remembered a time just like this before. It had been a week before her seventeenth birthday. He'd gotten them lift tickets and had driven her car up to Breckenridge for the day.

"You're quiet," he said as they made their way to the nearest hardware store.

"I was just remembering the time we went up to Breckinridge one Saturday to go skiing."

He smiled over at her. "We had a good time. I think I ended up with the flu?"

She laughed. "You did. Only because I'd forgotten my gloves…" She dropped off as she remembered he'd given her his gloves. Just like he'd done last night.

Sighing, she reached over and took his gloved hand in hers. "I guess I'm always forgetting them."

"It's a good thing I reminded you this time." He squeezed her gloved hand.

"Yes." She looked down at her cream-colored cotton-lined gloves. "I should have never doubted your reasons for leaving. I never even thought that there could be a bigger reason for you turning your back on everything you loved so dear."

"I did what I thought was best," he said softly.

"I know. At least now I do," she admitted. "You hurt me."

"And I'm willing to spend my entire life making it up to you," he promised with a smile.

Just hearing those words, she knew without a doubt that she would do anything to make that dream come true. Spending the rest of her life with him was all she could ever hope for.

CHAPTER 14

First thing Monday morning, Simon was called into a virtual meeting. He took the call in the conference room so as not to disturb Laura's work. She was once again on the phone trying to find workers to help move and set up all the furniture.

"What do you mean the permitting is backed up?" he asked Barbara.

"I mean, some man from the city stopped by the office this morning and told me that the permit had been placed on hold." Barbara replied.

"Did he say why?"

"No, just that you should give him a call on his direct line. I've forwarded you his name and number in the email I sent you earlier."

He pulled up the message and frowned at the contact.

"I thought we were working with Peter down at the permit office?" he asked her after seeing the name Max Duke with a number behind it.

"Yes, which is why I was thrown off when the man came into the office. Besides, he was… well, not very professional."

Simon felt his stomach sink as he looked at the name.

"I'll handle it from here," Simon said, guessing that he knew exactly who had stopped by his offices. Another one of his father's goons.

"Do you want me to give Peter a call?" Barbara asked.

"No." The sinking feeling in his gut grew. "I'll deal with it."

"Okay," Barbara said slowly. "If our permits fall through…"

"I know." He sighed. "I'll personally make sure everything goes through. Even if I have to head down to the office today myself." He added, "I'll keep you posted."

After hanging up with Barbara, he took a couple of deep breaths before punching the number for Max Duke.

"So, I hear you're back in town."

Simon knew the voice instantly and felt his anger grow.

"Dad," he spat out.

"Don't call me that," the man hissed.

"You know, I'm trying very hard to forget the fact that we have the same genes. You're the one holding onto that fact," he said smoothly.

"We had an agreement that you would never step foot in my state again," his father growled.

"It's not your state, and I never agreed to anything other than getting on a plane."

"You think you can play games with me? You know how much power I hold. I can make your life miserable."

"You'd hold up opening an orphanage just to keep your little secret?" Simon tried to keep his temper under check. After all, that's what the senator wanted. To get under his skin.

"You think you can come back into my territory? I know your kind. You're after what's mine. You think I'll play games with you, boy?" The man's voice rose and, by the time he was done talking, Simon had his phone a few inches from his ear. He knew his kind. Did that mean he had half-brothers or sisters out there? How many other women had he paid off to get rid of his problems?

"I'm not here for you. I'd die a happy man if I never saw or spoke to you again. I don't want anything from you. I never will. Stay out of my way and I'll stay out of yours," he said before hanging up on the man.

Instantly, his phone rang. Seeing the same number that he'd just called, he hit ignore and tossed his phone down on the table.

"Sorry," Laura's voice sounded from behind him. "I didn't mean to overhear…"

He turned towards her, and she rushed to his side.

"Is everything okay?" she asked, touching his shoulder.

"Yeah," he lied.

"Your father?" she asked.

"Yeah," he said again. He looked over at the phone when it rang again. When she moved to answer it, he stopped her. "Don't. He can't have what he wants."

"What is that?" she asked softly.

"To ruin me. I've worked too hard in the past five years for that to ever happen."

"Tell me what you need." She wrapped her arms around him.

"You," he answered after a moment, then he leaned down and placed his lips softly over hers.

"I'm here."

"So are we," a deep voice said from the doorway.

Simon turned to see Logan and Amy standing in the doorway, along with two other people.

"Shit," he thought, then realized he'd said it out loud. "Sorry, I thought the conference room was empty."

Logan smiled and motioned to the room. "It was at the time."

"Sorry." Simon picked up his still-ringing phone and hit ignore, then shoved it in his pocket. He glanced over to Laura, who was smiling at him. "We'll get out of your way." He took her hand and pulled her out of the room so that the group could use the room.

"Later," Amy said to Laura as they passed by. Laura nodded quickly before following him outside.

"Guess we'll have to be more careful around here," he said when they were back in her office.

She laughed. "Do you know how many times I've walked in on those two going at it?" She shook her head. "Trust me, the entire office has seen them kissing at one point."

He smiled and walked back over to wrap his arms around her. "Thanks."

"For?" she asked, looking up at him.

"For breaking me out of the funk my father caused."

"Any time." She leaned up and kissed him again. "What's he done now?"

"Threatened my permits."

Her eyes grew angry immediately.

"He can't do that." She jerked out of his arms. Then she marched over to her desk and picked up her phone.

"Get me David," she said into the phone. He waited, wanting to tell her to not bother, but figured it couldn't hurt. "David, Laura here, I hear permits for ReNewed Foster Facility are in jeopardy." She was quiet for a while. "Will you check on it for me? I have a personal stake in them going through. I know my uncle would be highly disappointed if our project was held up." She was silent again. "Yes, my mother was looking forward to it." She smiled and winked at him. "Thanks, David," she said before hanging up.

"Okay, want to tell me what that was all about?" He leaned on the edge of her desk.

"David Hopkins went to school with my uncle and mother. He's known my family forever. He's had the hots for my mom since grade school." She smiled. "He's the director down at the City of Golden offices." She touched his hand. "He's assured me that he will do everything in his power to make sure the permits go through and don't get held up."

It made him feel slightly better, but still, he knew how much pull a senator had over a director of the city. Money talked. It always had.

He'd spent a year looking into his father's business practices.

There were rumors about his father and, from what he'd found out, he knew most of those rumors were true. His father was as corrupt as they said. He didn't have proof that he'd rigged his elections, but the rest was so obvious to anyone who looked deep enough.

There were articles out there about his corruption, but then his father would donate or be connected to a charity and it was almost as if everyone just forgot the bad. It didn't matter how corrupt you were, just as long as you paid off the right people and occasionally did something positive.

Still, the reason Simon had finally returned to Colorado was that he knew that his bank account was easily double that of his father's at the moment.

Still, he hadn't thought about the power his father still wielded with his position. An oversight that could cost him everything.

"Relax," Laura said looking up into his eyes. "We'll get through this." She took his hand in hers. "Together."

For the rest of the week, the thought of losing everything hung over his head. Even when Laura moved a few of her things into his place and started spending each night in his bed, he worried.

It was four weeks before Christmas and every time they walked through a furniture store together, he was reminded by the plethora of decorations and the Christmas songs pumping through the speakers that his deadline was getting closer.

He was standing in the middle of one of three stores they'd

visited that day when he realized with a slight shock that he hadn't even purchased a gift for Laura yet.

"Something wrong?" Laura asked, stopping next to him.

"No," he quickly lied, and he continued to follow her throughout the store. He tried to come up with the perfect gift for her.

She stopped, and he almost bumped into her. "Oh, I forgot. I'm supposed to ask if you're free for Thanksgiving dinner tomorrow night. Logan and Amy want us at their place. My mother will be there." He noticed a slight glimmer in her eyes, but since he was so worried about what to get her, he just nodded his agreement.

How many years had he spent Thanksgiving with her family? He'd spent every single holiday at their house after he'd met Laura.

After he wrote yet another check for items she'd picked out at the store, she turned to him and dusted her hands.

"That's it," she said with a smile.

"What?" he asked with a slight frown.

"That's the last item we needed. Now we just have to wait for everything to be delivered and set up."

"What?" He glanced around. "Aren't there more..." He thought through everything they'd ordered or purchased in the last three weeks. "Beds?"

She smiled and shook her head. "No."

"Chairs? Tables? Something." He couldn't believe that she had ordered or found every single item that would fill the massive building that would be home to so many.

"It's all done. Well, ordered and purchased, at least. Now the real work begins. After it's all delivered, we have to assemble and set up everything." She smiled, then walked over and wrapped her arms around him. "How about we celebrate? Let's take the rest of the day off and do something... fun."

Instantly, his mind went to having her in bed again. He'd enjoyed falling asleep and waking up next to her all week long.

How had he gone five years without her? How could he ever imagine going another night without feeling her heartbeat? Hearing her soft breathing in the darkness of the night?

He was hooked. Addicted to her. Just like he'd been all those years ago.

"What do you say we head back, change out of our work clothes, and you let me take you for a night out?" he offered.

He knew he'd hit the mark when her smile doubled.

"That sounds amazing," she practically purred.

As they were walking out of the store, a tall blond man stopped them.

"Tom." Laura laughed and hugged the man. "I didn't expect to see you down here."

The man laughed and hugged her back. "Well, I do own the place."

"I know, it's just, I know Amber is in town right now."

He chuckled. "I'm meeting her here. She wanted to redecorate one of our extra bedrooms." He rolled his eyes. "I'm just thankful I own furniture stores."

Laura chuckled. "Oh, Tom, this is Simon."

Tom's eyes widened. "The Simon?"

"Afraid so," Simon said, taking Tom's outstretched hand and shaking it.

Tom chuckled. "You're the one opening up the foster care facility in the old Coors place?"

"Guilty," he said with a smile.

"We've heard a lot about you," Tom added, then the man's smile doubled as his eyes moved past him. "My wife." He walked over and wrapped his arms around a pretty blonde woman that Simon had seen in several movies.

Amber Scott was as drop-dead gorgeous in real life as she

was on the screen. Still, she had nothing on Laura, he thought as Tom introduced them.

"We won't keep you long," Amber said after a few moments of chatter.

"I hear you're redecorating a guest room?" Laura said. "You know, I could help out if you need ideas about colors or design?"

Amber's smile grew. "I think we'll be okay." She glanced up at Tom. "I've decided to paint the room pink." Her words hung in the air for a moment, then Tom let out a whoop and scooped up his wife and spun her in a circle.

"Okay, what'd we…" Laura's words dropped off. "You're pregnant?" she asked, almost squealing.

"Yup," Tom answered with a smile. "We were supposed to find out the sex and do a whole party, but…" He looked down at Amber. "This was more our style."

"Wow, congratulations," Laura added. "You'll be joining…" She bit her bottom lip and then shook her head. "Sorry," she said, clearing her throat.

"Oh no, you don't." Amber narrowed her eyes at Laura. "Who? Spill." She crossed her arms over her chest.

He looked down at Laura and knew instantly by the way her cheeks had turned a shade of bright pink that she had a secret.

"I promised not to tell…" Laura started, but then she leaned closer to Amber. "Don't tell anyone, but last week Amy found out that she's pregnant. She's going to tell my brother tomorrow night. When the entire family is around."

"Oh, how wonderful!" Amber hugged Laura. "Cousins, of sorts." She laughed. "Since Amy and Kristen act like sisters."

"True," Laura agreed. "You two have fun decorating your nursery."

"If we need any help, I'll call you," Amber said as they started walking out.

"I bet you could have your own business up and running in

no time. All you'd have to do is hang around the furniture store and advertise," he joked as he helped her into the car.

"I've already talked to Logan briefly about it. He agreed that if I do start my own interior design business that he would make it a requirement that each sale that RMR closed would get my information."

He chuckled. "I guess it does pay to have friends or family in the right places."

CHAPTER 15

*C*hanging out of her painting clothes and trying to find a dress suitable for a snowy evening out, she thought about her own future.

For the first time since Simon had returned, she hoped. Dreamed. Thought about what her own family could be like in a few years.

She'd always dreamed of having a life with him, at least she had when she'd been younger. Then he'd left and her future had been a big black hole.

Now that he was back, that spot was starting to fill in again. The more time they spent together, the more she hoped.

She pulled on a cream-colored sweater dress and added dark brown stockings, her high tan boots, and a matching belt to the ensemble. She double-checked her reflection in the long mirror in her small bedroom.

She'd moved a few necessary things over to Simon's place, but still, most of her clothing was at her apartment. Looking around her small space, she realized she hadn't even taken the time to turn her one-bedroom apartment into anything close to resembling a home. Sure, she had a few items here and there, but if anyone looked, they would see that her heart hadn't been in decorating her own space.

Simon had agreed to pick her up in an hour, which gave her plenty of time to finish changing. She even had time to pull out the Christmas present that she'd started their last year together. She hadn't worked on it since he'd left.

It was funny bringing the large thing out of storage after he'd returned. Now, it sat tucked in the back of her closet, hiding from him in case he ever visited her place.

Pulling out the heavy wood board now, she stared down at the many images of their faces pasted together on the large board.

Maybe she should have thrown the thing out years ago, but every time she thought to do so, something had stopped her.

She'd put too much into it. Into him. Somehow, she thought of the massive board with more than three dozen pictures of them in various ages as more than just a gift she'd made for him.

It was their life. A history of their love. It showcased every step they had taken in life, from friends to lovers. She couldn't have thrown it away any more than she could have given up on the hope that one day he'd return to her.

When there was a knock on the door, she shoved the thing back into her closet and rushed to open it.

A dark figure stood in her doorway, and she was about to slam the door when the figure turned towards her and she realized that it was a woman in a suit.

"Miss Miller? Mr. Berg sent the car for you. I'm your driver for the night." The woman smiled and motioned towards the parking lot where a large dark limo sat waiting. Simon stood just outside the car, holding a large bundle of cheerful yellow daisies in his hands. Her favorite flowers.

She grabbed her long black coat, gloves, and purse and followed the driver down the stairs to the parking lot.

"You look beautiful." Simon smiled and held out the flowers for her.

It had been snowing since noon that day and now the flakes had turned bigger and wetter. His dark hair was slicked back, and white specks melted in it and dampened it even further. He wore a thick wool black coat and his black leather gloves. He was wearing black slacks and shoes but she couldn't see if he was wearing a sweater or a dress shirt under the thick wool coat.

"Thank you." She buried her face into the flowers and enjoyed the scent of spring during the chill.

"Shall we?" He opened the door for her himself.

She slid onto the leather seats and held onto the flowers while he climbed in beside her.

"There's a vase." He grabbed up a glass filled with water beads. "This should hold them over until we get back."

She set the flowers in the vase and set them down on the seat next to her. "They're beautiful. I'll be honest, I didn't think you'd remembered my favorite flowers until you brought me some at the café."

He chuckled. "Some things I'd forgotten, but it's all coming back to me." He took her gloved hands in his as the car started moving.

"Where are we going?" she asked, feeling slightly nervous all of a sudden.

"I thought we'd head up into the mountains. I remembered how much you liked that place in Idaho Springs."

She laughed. "Beau Jo's?"

"That's the one. I know it's not a fancy—"

"It's perfect. I haven't been there in years."

In fact, the last time she'd been up there had been a month before he'd left. Somehow, even the restaurant had been tainted after he'd left.

"Good. If you want to go someplace else…" he started.

"Simon, it is perfect. I haven't been back there since the last time we were there together," she admitted.

"Really?" His dark eyebrows went up slightly.

"Yeah." She smiled at him. "Some things just didn't seem right… alone."

"Didn't you have anyone else?"

She laughed. "No, no one. Just you."

He hugged her. "Me too. I know it's probably terrible of me to say so, but I'm thankful."

She laughed. "I am too."

"No one seemed compelling after you," he admitted, and she realized she felt the same way.

None of the men she'd tried to date after he'd left had seemed interesting. Not that she'd tried very hard. She'd been focused on classes and work.

"Have you heard anything more about the permits?" she asked, trying to fight off the nerves.

He sighed and wrapped his arm around her shoulders. "Not yet. As far as anyone down at the office knows, we're on track."

"That's good. When can we start setting everything up?"

"Laura." He took her hands in his, then slowly removed both of their gloves. "Let's not fill our free time with work talk. Tell me something about yourself that I don't know." He reached up and brushed a finger down her chin. "Something new. Pretend this is our first date."

She chuckled nervously. "Somehow, it already feels like it. Even though I know everything there is to know about you, I'm nervous."

"Don't be," he said softly, taking her hand in his. "Remember our first date?"

She thought about it and laughed. "You were nervous then."

He smiled. "I was so nervous that I think I sweat through three shirts before I showed up and knocked on your door."

She smiled and relaxed. "I had changed outfits twice myself.

Not because I sweat through them, but because I was nervous about where you were going to take me."

"How many outfits did you go through tonight?" he asked, running a hand over the soft sweater dress.

"Just one. You?"

"Same," he said with a smile. "Now, it did take me at least half an hour to do my hair." He reached up and ran his fingers through the now-dry locks.

She laughed and realized she was completely relaxed now.

"God, I missed you," she admitted with a sigh. "You were my best friend. The only person who could make me feel nervous and relaxed at the same time. The only person I could tell everything to."

"You still can. I've missed you too. Growing up in foster care could have been very lonely for me, but I had you and your family every step of the way. The best day of my life was when you walked into Mrs. Humphrey's classroom."

She smiled. "I lucked out when the only empty seat was right next to the cutest boy in class." She touched his cheek.

"Now I want to turn this limo around and head back to my place," he said against her lips.

"Too bad, you already said the magic word. Pizza." She smiled and pulled away from him. "Besides, I'm starving."

"Yeah." He sighed and ran his hands through his hair again, a move that meant he was frustrated, she remembered. "Tell me something about you that I missed while I was gone," he said, and she could tell that he was trying to change the subject.

"I graduated college with a four-point three." She knew she'd throw him off.

His eyebrows shot up. "You did?"

She nodded and smiled. "Logan claims it's because I took all the easy classes."

He chuckled. "He's just jealous. If I remember correctly, you were always smarter than he was."

She chuckled. "I've been telling him that since first grade."

He took her hand again and lifted it to his lips as the limo weaved up the snowy mountain roads. "I'm so thankful I had you. It's my Christmas wish to give that to other kids that are going through what I went through back then."

Her hand tightened on his. "You are amazing."

"No, I'm selfish. If I were amazing, I'd adopt every kid out there."

She laughed. "You'd need a bigger house."

He smiled. "Yeah. Someday we'll have a house full of kids and maybe some dogs running us both crazy."

Her smiled doubled. Just hearing him say those words warmed her heart beyond anything else he could have said to her.

"I like dogs," she said, and he laughed.

She couldn't remember having a more perfect night with Simon. They ate their pizza as they overlooked the snow-covered main street of the small mountain town of Idaho Springs. After, they took a stroll down the street and enjoyed all the Christmas lights and the massive, decorated tree in the center of town. There were people huddled around, singing carols and handing out hot chocolate.

When they became too cold to stay outside any longer, they headed back.

By the time they climbed into the limo to take them down the hill, she was exhausted and happily numb from the cold.

She rested her head on his shoulder as they started down the mountain slowly, and she realized that she had never had a more perfect time in her life.

"This was a perfect night," she said with a sigh. "It was a good idea to get a driver. I remember the last time we drove in the mountains on a snowy night." She held in a laugh.

His chest vibrated with a chuckle.

"I'd only driven a handful of times back then," he admitted.

"You did great. It was all the other crazy drivers that I was worried about." She glanced up at him, enjoying the sight of his strong profile shadowed in the dark car.

"Laura." He lifted her chin with his finger until their eyes locked. "I—"

His arms quickly tightened around her when they heard the high piercing sound of tires squealing and then a loud bang of metal against metal.

Laura was thrown around the back of the limo as she screamed and tried desperately to hold onto Simon. The back of her head connected with something solid, which shattered, cutting into her skin. Ice-cold water washed over her entire body. Moments later she was jerked into complete darkness as she lost consciousness.

CHAPTER 16

Simon's grip on Laura tightened as he fought for a way out of the back of the sinking limo. He was thankful she was unconscious so she wouldn't panic. There was only room enough for one of them to lose their shit in the back of the dark limo.

The best he could figure, the driver had lost control on the snowy roads and had gone over the edge, landing them in the Clear Creek, which ran along the highway at parts.

His eyes moved up to the front of the limo, where the dark glass separated the back section from the front. He didn't know if the driver had gotten out or if she was even still alive.

At the rate the water was coming into the back of the car, he doubted he would have time to check if they were going to get out with their own lives.

He climbed up to the rear door, holding tight to Laura's unconscious body, and tried the door handle.

Thankfully, the door popped open easily and almost flew off its hinges because of gravity since the back of the car was in the air. He braced for more water to rush in the opening and when it didn't, he figured only the front of the car was submerged at this point since the car was pointing into the river.

Climbing out of the back of the limo while holding Laura was extremely challenging.

"Hello?" someone called from somewhere above them. "I've called for help."

Suddenly, a bright light shone on him.

"My god, do you need help?" someone else called out. "I've got a rope."

He shifted Laura in his arms and sat on the edge of the door frame, holding onto her. He felt the cold intensify when the wind blew past him. They'd gotten soaked, and he reached down with shaky hands to feel Laura's skin. He felt for her pulse and relaxed a little when he felt it under his fingertips but frowned at how cold she was already.

"Here," someone said directly above him. "Let me take her." A young man dressed in grey overalls stood on the trunk of the limo, a thick yellow rope wrapped around his waist. "We'll get her up the hill."

"I'm going to check on the driver," he said, handing Laura's unconscious body over to the man.

"Better not," the man said. "The front of the car is underwater. I doubt the man survived."

"It's a woman," Simon said as he disappeared back into the limo.

He held himself up by the edge of the seat and shimmied his way to the front window. There was no sound coming from the front of the car and that worried him.

He tried to roll the thick black glass between the two sections down by using the switch, but when nothing happened, he started banging on the glass.

Then he noticed a small crack at the top of the glass and pried his fingers between the space and pulled it the rest of the way down.

Even more icy water rushed into the back compartment until it was up to his waist. He hissed in his breath as he searched the darkness of the front seat.

Seeing the woman's mangled body and her clear eyes staring back at him under a foot of the freezing water, he decided there was nothing he could do for her. If he didn't get back out of the car now, he might end up going down with it. Or freezing himself.

It took all his strength to climb back up the inside of the limo. His limbs were numb by the time he crawled out the back door again.

"There he is!" someone shouted.

"Here." The man in the overalls was back, his hand stretched out for Simon's.

"Laura?" he asked as he took the man's hand.

"She's up there, asking for you." The man nodded to where all the lights were above them.

"Shit, it's cold," Simon said between chattering teeth.

"The driver?" the man asked quietly.

"Gone," Simon said, feeling his heart sink. "Looks like she died on impact."

"Shit," the man said as he helped Simon climb up the embankment.

The moment they reached the mangled guardrail, a thick blanket was tossed over his shoulders.

"Here, come sit in my car until the ambulance arrives," someone said. "Your girl is waiting for you."

He was half carried, half dragged to the back of a white SUV. The moment he sat down in the back seat, Laura was there, wrapping her arms around him.

"I thought…" she cried and held onto him. "When I woke up, you weren't there," she said, her wet hair plastered to her face.

"I'm sorry," he said, holding onto her. "I had to try…" He closed his eyes for a moment.

The car's heater pumped warm air over them, but not even that and the dry blanket and Laura's arms around him could chase away the chill he felt, knowing a life had just been lost.

"I'm sorry," he said again as tears rolled down his frozen cheeks.

The moment the ambulance arrived, they were shuffled into the back of it where they stripped off their wet clothes and were wrapped in heat blankets.

A police officer sat in the back with them and asked them more than a dozen questions, none of which they had answers to. He relayed what he'd witnessed, which matched what Laura had gone through up to the point where the vase of flowers had somehow hit her in the back of the head, causing her to lose consciousness.

He was surprised when a witness knocked on the back door and relayed that a large black truck had sideswiped the limo, forcing it off the road. They didn't get the license plate number but had a pretty good description of the truck.

They were shuttled in the ambulance to the nearest hospital, which happened to be the one in Golden. Laura had used someone's cell phone to call her family and by the time they got there, Logan and Amy were waiting for them with a bag of dry clothes.

He sat beside her while the doctor examined her head and then waited as she was shuffled out of the room for a CT scan.

Thankfully, an hour later they were both cleared, and Logan drove them back up to his place. By then, it was close to one in the morning.

"Sorry about this," Laura said to Logan as she hugged him after they climbed out of the car. The snow had stopped falling, but still Simon couldn't seem to get warm enough.

"I'm just thankful you two are okay," Logan said as he hugged Laura. He reached over and shook Simon's hand. "Thanks for saving my sister tonight."

"I didn't…" he started, but the man wrapped his arms around him.

"I overheard the cop relaying the story. You saved her. So, thanks." He smiled and then glanced at Laura. "We'll see both of you at our place for Thanksgiving dinner."

The first thing he did when they stepped into the house was wrap his arms around Laura and hold onto her. Feeling her shiver, he hoisted her up into his arms and carried her into his bathroom.

"I feel like the only thing that can warm me is you," he said as he gently pulled their borrowed clothes off them. He stepped under the hot spray with her body pressed against his, and his control slipped. He started to show her just how he felt about her.

It was as if his hands moved on their own accord, taking what he needed from her while enjoying those sexy little pleasure sounds that she made. The more his need grew, the more demanding he was. He pushed her against the tile wall, hoisted her up, and pinned her between him and the wall as he fully embedded himself into her heat.

There had never been anything equal to the pleasure she gave him. Her skin felt so wonderful rubbing up against his, the feeling of her breasts in his hands, her lips sliding over his own. It was all so much, but he kept trying to wait for the signs that she'd gotten to her pleasure. Only when he felt her tighten around him and cry out his name did he allow himself to let go of everything.

"That was a first." Laura sighed against his shoulder.

"Hm?" he asked, holding them both up against the shower wall.

"First time in the shower." She leaned her head back and rested it on the tile. He noticed her wince when she bumped the spot on the back of her head where the vase had connected.

"You're hurting." He gathered her up again and sat on the shower bench with her in his lap.

"I'm fine." She smiled up at him. "Just tired." She rested her head against his, and he realized there was still a little dried blood in her hair. For the next few minutes, he carefully shampooed her hair, removing all the caked blood from her long blonde locks.

"I could just fall asleep here, in your arms," she said with a sign.

"Then do. I'll take care of you," he promised as he used the sprayer to rinse the shampoo from her hair.

"Hmm, I'm sort of hungry." She glanced up at him. "You don't happen to have any chocolate in the house, do you?"

He chuckled and nodded, then quickly scooped her up and turned off the water.

He enjoyed drying her with the oversized towels that had been one of his first purchases for the place.

"Here." He pulled out a pair of his sweats and handed them to her, then pulled on another pair himself. "You relax back. I'll go hunt us up some chocolate."

She didn't waste any time. After pulling on the sweats, she crawled under the blankets and pulled them up to her chin.

"I'll start a fire in here first." He sidetracked and lit a fire in the fireplace. He'd warmed up a little, but still, it was as if his core was a few degrees too low. Warming his hands for a moment to make sure the fire took off, he glanced over and noticed that Laura was watching him.

"Thanks," she said softly, "for saving me."

He smiled and felt his heart swell with love. "Any time."

Ten minutes later, he walked back into the bedroom holding a tray of mugs filled with hot chocolate and a bowl of chocolate mousse topped with cool whip.

Her entire face was under the covers.

"You okay in there?" he asked, pulling back the blankets.

She cracked open her eyes and nodded. "I'm still so cold."

He touched her forehead and realized she was burning up.

"Yeah, the doctor said you might have a fever after the mild hypothermia." Thankfully, he had the Tylenol ready. The doctor had mentioned they both might need to take some.

"What about you?" she asked through chattering teeth.

"I feel fine," he lied and figured he'd take a Tylenol with his hot chocolate.

"Mmm," she said when she noticed the mugs. "Hot cocoa?" She sat up, bringing the blankets with her.

He handed her the mug and then took his own and clicked it against hers. "To cheating death," he said soberly.

"To life," she corrected. "And all the years still ahead of us."

"I like that better. I love you," he said after taking a sip and making sure she'd swallowed the pill.

"I love you too. But if you don't get in this bed and warm me up soon, I may have to crawl over to the fireplace." She smiled. "Or get a dog to snuggle up to."

He chuckled and made sure not to spill his drink as he crawled under the blankets with her.

Once her head was back on his shoulder and they were watching the fire from across the room, he sighed.

They sat for a moment, listening to the hiss and crackle of the logs burning in the fireplace. The soothing sound lulled him and allowed him to think.

She broke into the silence. "Do you think it was your father's doing?"

He'd been thinking the same thing. If it wasn't his father, it was an uncanny coincidence.

"I'm determined to get to the bottom of it. Regardless." He thought about the driver's family. Somewhere, someone was getting a visit from the police about their daughter, sister, or mother not coming home, and he was pretty sure it was all his fault.

CHAPTER 17

They spent as much of the following day in bed as they could. At one point, after he'd made them grilled cheese sandwiches and tomato soup for lunch, they'd showered and dressed for dinner at her brother's.

She still felt a little groggy, and her head hurt when she tried to comb and style her hair, but she kept telling herself that she was extremely lucky to be alive. Just thinking that the woman who'd stood on her doorstep last night to greet her hadn't been so lucky had her appreciating every ache.

Thanksgiving dinner at her brother's was a quiet event. They were there to celebrate everything they were thankful for and for the announcement of Amy's pregnancy.

Laura tried to put on a happy face. She smiled and laughed along with her family. But under it all, she kept replaying the night before. Replaying the fact that Simon's father could very well be behind the death of the driver.

When the subject was brought up by Logan, Simon informed them all that his security on them would be doubled.

"I let my guard down for one night and, because of it, someone won't be spending the holidays with her family today.

Won't be spending Christmas with the people she loves." He glanced over at her. "I don't know what I would have done if anything had happened to Laura." He squeezed her hand and then glanced around the room. "Or any of you."

"Do you think the senator would go to such great lengths?" her mother asked Simon.

Simon shrugged. "I'm not willing to take the risk," he said, then turned back to her. "I was hoping that, at least..." He cleared his throat and his face heated. "Not how I wanted to do this, but I was hoping you'd move in with me."

She smiled and felt her heart jump. "Of course, I will."

His dark eyebrows shot up. "Today?"

She laughed. "You can hire a moving company. I'll have to break my lease."

"Done," he said quickly and hugged her.

"Now, let's celebrate." Amy stood up and disappeared into the kitchen, then came back with a large cake. The evening returned to the lighter mood and she was thankful for her family. Thankful for everything she had.

"I can help you move some of your things over to Simon's place tomorrow," Logan suggested.

Her eyebrows shot up. "You're going to help me? Move?"

Logan nudged her toe under the table. "If I remember correctly, I moved all of your stuff last time."

She smiled. "That's because the time before that, you abandoned me."

Logan laughed. "We were on our honeymoon."

"Excuses." She rolled her eyes as she smiled. Then she quickly added, "I'll take the help."

"I could probably rustle up some other help. Aiden and the guys," Logan said with a shrug.

"We can hire..." Simon started to say.

"I don't have that much stuff," she admitted. "Your bed is better than the one I have, so mine can be sold or hauled down to the junkyard." She shrugged. "I have a few nice things that could benefit your place, but other than that, I hadn't focused on getting nice things. Not while I was stuck renting. There was never any use."

"If you're sure?" Simon asked her.

"I am." She relaxed. "Actually, most of my things are still in boxes from my last move. I only moved into my apartment four months ago."

Then she wondered how she was going to move Simon's Christmas gift. She'd have to sneak it past him and find a place to hide it until she could finish the thing. She'd taken a few pictures of them last night when they'd been in Idaho Springs and had wanted to get them printed out. Now, however, she didn't want those memories to be the focus. A woman had lost her life shortly after they'd had such an enjoyable time.

As Simon drove them back to his place, she wondered about the driver.

"Do you think you can find out about the limo driver? It would be nice to do something for her family," she said as she watched the rain fall.

The snow had all but melted away during the warm day and now the rain washed away the last of the sand that had been laid out on the roads.

"Yeah, I've already put in a call to find out," he said as they pulled in front of the garage. "When I find out, we'll make sure to do something. Together." He shut off the engine.

"Simon, I'm thankful that you were there for me. I don't know what I would've done…"

"You wouldn't have been put in that position if I wasn't there," he said in a low tone.

"Hey." She took his hand in hers. "You can't blame yourself for what happened. The blame lies solely on whoever caused the accident." She searched his eyes.

She noticed the moment he gave up the fight and nodded. "I know you're right." He leaned over and kissed her.

That night, in his arms, she thought about what she could do to show him how much it meant to her that he was back in her life. So far, since he'd returned, she'd tried to fight off the attraction and had made him jump through hoops to win her back, but the truth was, he'd never lost her.

All these years that she'd been waiting for him, she'd still considered herself his. She would always be his.

The following day was filled with boxes and moving. She'd texted her brother early that morning and asked him to move the picture board over to his place. She'd given him a spare key to her place when she'd moved in, and he'd run over and had it removed before she and Simon arrived to start moving her things.

Once they'd moved all of her small items over to the big house, she decided that there wasn't anything else worth saving and scheduled a local charity to come to pick up the rest of her things.

"For someone so good at decorating homes, I would have thought that you'd want to hang onto more of your things," Simon said once he unloaded the last of her boxes into the house.

"I never really got into decorating for myself," she admitted. "I always spent my extra money on clothes instead."

He chuckled. "I remember you have a clothes addiction."

She nudged his shoulder. "Take that back," she teased. "It's not an addiction so much as a hobby."

He laughed. "Right." He motioned to all the boxes sitting in front of the large walk-in closet. "These are all clothes, right?"

She laughed. "Okay, it's an addiction."

He pulled her into his arms. "So, now that you're here, I have some rules." He pulled out a small key ring and dangled it in front of her.

She laughed. "Okay, shoot."

"I get the left side of the bed." He frowned. "Or the right side... I guess it depends on where you're at. Whatever side you're on, that's where I'll be."

She smiled. "Anything else?"

He nodded. "I'll expect you to conserve water..."

She laughed. "Meaning... we'll shower together?"

"Exactly." He chuckled.

"Then we should carpool as well," she suggested.

"Now you're getting it." He leaned down and kissed the tip of her nose. "Welcome home," he said softly.

For the rest of the weekend, he helped her unpack all of her things. Since the main bedroom closet was massive, there was plenty of room for her things next to his.

When they were done unloading the boxes, she talked him into working on painting the dining room. It was a god-awful shade of mint green and needed to be the next to receive fresh paint.

She'd chosen a soft grey, and had decided to paint the wainscoting white again.

By the time they were done Sunday evening, the room looked brand new and very modern. She even found a few pictures among her things that accented the colors, and they hung up in the room.

First thing Monday morning, they headed down to the facility. The hope was that they would be overseeing the work on assembling all the furniture. That is if the place passed the final inspection, which was set for that morning.

When they arrived, she busied herself with overseeing the delivery from Albert's Furniture, making sure each piece went in the correct room. She hadn't realized just how much they'd ordered until another massive truck arrived after they had finished unloading the first semi.

When Simon found her, she was opening a box that looked

like it had been dropped to ensure that the lamp inside hadn't been damaged.

"So?" she asked him. "Did we pass?"

He shrugged. "With a few minor adjustments they're making now on the electric in the office, and the HVAC getting some adjustments, yes."

She squealed and hugged him. "Congratulations. Does this mean we can start unpacking for real?"

"This was the CO. Our certificate of occupancy. We can technically unload and start setting everything up. We haven't officially received approval for our certificate of family foster care yet. The kids and staff won't be able to move in until we do."

"So, what I'm hearing is… I can get to work?" she asked with a smile.

He chuckled. "Have at it." He motioned towards the boxes. "I'll call for backup and have a crew here to help out."

"Thanks." She lifted up to her toes and kissed him.

"Thank *you*. Now, what do you need help with?"

They spent most of their time that day unpackaging items. When the crew arrived and started putting bed frames and furniture together, she stood back and directed the work and answered questions. At one point, Simon disappeared and came back with a sandwich and coffee for her. They sat out on one of the new balconies overlooking the grounds and ate lunch.

"There's going to be a soccer field there. The playground and basketball courts will be there." He pointed out each section. "I'm even thinking of creating a skate park."

She laughed. "I remember the one time you tried to skateboard."

He groaned. "Okay, so just because I'm not good at something doesn't mean that other kids aren't."

She reached over and took his hand in hers. "This is all so amazing." She felt her heart swell.

He looked down at their joined hands. "I found out the name of our driver," he said, avoiding her eyes. "Kayla Smith." He glanced up at her. "She was a single mother to a two-year-old daughter named Lilith. Kayla was working two jobs just to pay rent on her tiny one-bedroom place off Colfax."

Laura felt tears flood her eyes. "What will happen to Lilith?" she asked, her heart breaking for the little girl.

"The authorities are looking for Kayla's family."

"Where is the girl now?" she asked, her heart going out to a little girl who had just lost her entire world.

"Right now? Foster care." He sighed.

"Simon." She touched his hand. "What can we do to help?"

He looked around and nodded. "We're doing it. Getting this place open is our highest priority. When I hear more about the situation, I'll see if we can have her moved here."

Laura shook her head. "That's not good enough." She wiped a tear from her face. "Somehow, we're responsible."

"I know," he said softly. "I'll see what else can be done."

"Thank you." She closed her eyes and took a deep breath of the winter air. She could tell instantly that they were due for more snow. Lots of it, according to the chilly northern breeze.

Just the thought of that little two-year-old spending Christmas in foster care broke Laura's heart. She'd been there when her mother had died. If only she hadn't lost consciousness. She could have crawled out of the limo herself while Simon had helped Kayla.

Her mind raced at all the possibilities as her heart ached for the little girl who was now all alone in the world.

Over the next two weeks, he and Laura spent the majority of their time down at the facility. She'd started on the bedrooms on the third floor and slowly worked her way down to the staff areas.

By the beginning of the second week, he moved Barbara and the rest of the staff over to help setup their own spaces.

Every day when he walked through the front doors of the facility, he was surprised at how quickly the place was coming together. The staff had started decorating for the holiday grand-opening party they were planning for the children.

The new security system had a few bugs to work out and, on several occasions, the police or fire department had shown up without the system going off. But this served as a way for them to share the grand opening to the crews, who happily spread the news to their families and friends.

The party was going to be complete with a jolly Santa Claus, played by himself, and a huge sleigh.

He'd spent a few nights online with Laura, picking out presents for each of the kids that were scheduled to move into the facility two days before Christmas.

They were still waiting for the final approval on the certificate of foster care, and he'd pulled as many strings as he could so the entire thing didn't unravel in front of his face.

He'd heard from the Colorado foster care offices that the senator had called and voiced his concerns about the facility, but Kimberly Stifle, the head of the department, had gotten on the line and assured him that she didn't give a rat's ass—her words, not his—what that no-good son of a bitch thought anyway.

He immediately invited the woman to the grand-opening event. She'd graciously accepted, and he planned on getting the woman the largest fruit and flower basket he could find as a thank you.

Which brought him back to why he was standing in the middle of a jewelry store searching for Laura's gift when he'd lied to her and told her he was at a meeting across town.

The woman behind the counter was being extremely patient with him, but the fact was, there were just too many rings to choose from.

He'd probably screwed up when he'd told her the amount that he was willing to spend. She had practically drooled. She'd offered him wine or champagne, which he'd turned down since he would be returning to help set up the family rooms after he was done picking up a ring.

He grew frustrated at the massive, overpriced rocks that she kept showing him and was about to walk out of the store when a simple elegant silver ring and square-cut diamond caught his eye.

"What about this one?" he asked the woman, who quickly turned her nose up at it.

"Oh, I think we can do much better than this simple thing. I mean, it's nice and all, but..." She pulled it from the case and frowned. "It's not even in your budget."

He misunderstood at first and believed the ring to be more

expensive than the number he'd given the woman. But when he took the ring from her fingers and held it up to the light, he caught a glance at the price and smiled. It was *below* his budget. It was perfect. The simple lines, the clearness of the main diamond, which was surrounded by smaller stones. He couldn't get over how beautiful it was and how perfectly it would fit Laura.

"Is there a wedding band that goes with it?" he asked.

"Yes." The woman went back to the display case and came up with a simple band studded with smaller stones.

"I'll take it," he said with a smile as the woman deflated at the prospect of her large commission shrinking.

Glancing down at the display case, he noticed a matching tennis bracelet and pointed. "And that bracelet and matching earrings as well."

The woman's smile grew. "Yes, sir."

Fifteen minutes later, he walked out of the store with the complete set, each individually wrapped in white wrapping paper held together with a blue bow.

Stashing the items in his glove box, he drove towards the facility and parked next to Laura's car.

He had needed to run errands first thing that morning, so they had ridden separately for the first time. That had given him the idea to hit the jewelry store before heading back to help her out after lunch.

He walked into the main office area and found Barbara unloading boxes of paperwork.

"How's it going in here?" he asked her as he set a box of cookies that he'd purchased for the office down on the counter.

"Good, these are the last boxes." She glanced up and smiled. "Are those cookies?" She got up and opened the lid. "God, I need these." She grabbed up a cookie and bit into it. "I was running low on energy."

He smiled. "I figured you would be." He glanced around. "Is Laura helping you out?"

"She went upstairs to start unpackaging the tables in the family meeting rooms about an hour ago." Barbara turned back to her work.

When he turned to go, she stopped him. "You might want to take a few of those up there. I don't think she stopped for lunch today."

He frowned as he took a couple of cookies and put them on a plate to carry up to Laura.

When he stepped onto the second-floor landing, he could hear the banging of workers putting the bunk beds together on the third floor. It was the last of the work to be done in the children's rooms before the kids could be moved in.

The main kids' hangout areas on the second floor were already finished. The theater room, with its massive flat screen television, leather theater-style recliners, and game consoles, which he'd setup himself, was one of his favorite rooms. There were two other rooms on the second floor and a library on the main floor that had been filled with donated books.

The kitchen staff was busy on the main floor preparing planned meals for his and the staff's approval. Honestly, he couldn't wait to try a few dishes. If the smells coming out of the kitchen were any hint, he may end up taking meals there himself. Laura had even joked about it herself.

He stuck his head into what would be one of the family meeting areas. There were four such rooms, each one bright and cheery, where families could meet and spend time with prospective foster children. He frowned at the large boxes that had yet to be unpacked.

After poking his head into each of the four family rooms and not finding Laura, he searched the entire second floor, then moved up to the third floor, where there were a handful of men working to put together the bunk beds.

When he noticed that Lee, the man he'd been concerned about earlier, was one of them, his worry for Laura's safety doubled. He'd looked into the man after that first day. He wanted to know everything about the guy. There was something about the man that Simon couldn't put his finger on. The man technically worked for Joe McCaw's company, but that hadn't stopped Simon from checking him out.

"Have you seen Laura?" he asked one of the other crew quietly.

"Nope, not since before lunch," the man said as he finished carrying a large piece of one of the beds into another room.

Pulling out his cell phone, Simon punched Laura's number and frowned when the call went instantly to voicemail.

Rushing back downstairs, he asked Barbara and her crew to help him search the facility for her. He took the rooms on the main floor while Barbara and the other office workers headed back upstairs to double-check for her.

Half an hour later, he was positive that Laura was no longer in the building. He continued to call her cell phone, but each time it went directly to her voicemail. It was as if the phone had been switched off.

Since her car was still in the parking lot, he knew that she hadn't left the facility on her own. Besides, his security detail was still watching the facility from the parking lot, as if she was somewhere inside.

He walked over to confirm that with the two men he'd hired as security. Normally, if she was at work or home, they would have taken off, but since the night of the limo, he'd kept someone on her twenty-four hours a day.

"She went inside around nine and hasn't come back out. You've said yourself you didn't want us to be underfoot inside the building," Evan, one of the security men said. "We haven't seen her leave yet."

"Besides," the other guy said, "her car is still there." He

motioned to Laura's car, which Simon had parked next to less than half an hour earlier.

He asked them to join in the search and then walked by her car. He noticed that her doors were still locked. He decided to call Logan to see if he'd heard from her recently.

"I'm sure she's around there someplace. The place is massive. Have you checked each room?" Logan asked.

"I have. Logan, I think you need to come down here. I'm afraid something bad has happened. We need to get everyone looking."

"I'll be there in fifteen," Logan said before hanging up.

Simon walked back to the main door, then sidetracked and decided to walk around the building instead. It was a massive place, which is why he knew it would be perfect for what he wanted to do. There was plenty of outside space for the kids to play.

The snow over the past few days had left more than half a foot in some places. There was a tall snowdrift near the back door. It had to be shoveled each morning, as the wind pushed it across the pathway every night.

Besides the front and back doors, there were two more doorways. One was at the loading docks for the kitchen area, and the other left from the side of the building to what would become the playground and sports areas.

Seeing footprints in the snow, he decided to follow them out into the field. He could have sworn there were two prints, one small boot inside a larger one, but they were too melted from the sun that hit the field to be sure.

Making a point not to disturb the prints, he followed them towards a large garage that sat against the hillside. It would eventually house all of the sports and lawn equipment, once spring allowed any of the work outside to be done.

Since he hadn't purchased any equipment yet, the garage

door sat unlocked. Sliding it open, he glanced around the dark room and waited for his eyes to adjust.

He thought he heard something, some kind of movement, and stepped into the darkness before his eyes could fully adjust.

"Laura?" he called out and almost jumped when a bird flew towards him and out the open door. "Shit." He held his hand over his heart in hopes that it would settle back down. "Laura?" he called out again, this time prepared for any other birds to bombard him.

He blinked a few times as his eyes adjusted, and he moved further into the darkness.

He spotted the dark mound and raced across the space, kneeling beside the dirty blanket. His fingers shook as he pulled it aside.

Seeing her pale blue skin, he cried out and gathered her into his arms. She was freezing. She wasn't even wearing a coat or gloves. Had someone stashed her there, in hopes that she would freeze to death?

Quickly, he removed his coat and covered her before lifting her into his arms and rushing back to the building.

He must have jostled her awake, because she groaned and cried out his name.

"I'm here," he said softly between puffs of breath as he ran to get her back into the warmth.

When he came to the back door, he realized that it was locked from the inside. It would take too long to run around the building, so he kicked the door and yelled as he pulled out his phone to call Barbara.

Before she could answer, the door flew open and one of the staff stood there looking at him with concern.

"What happened?" the woman asked.

"Get me some blankets and call the police," he said, rushing past her.

He gently laid Laura down on the sofa in the main room and

covered her in the blankets someone had provided. He took Laura's hands in his and rubbed them and her arms, willing his warmth into her.

Laura's eyes were open now, and she was staring at him as if she couldn't understand what was going on.

"Hypothermia," he warned the room. "She needs..." He stopped when he heard the ambulance. Picking her up gently, he rushed her outside to the waiting ambulance.

He sat back as the EMTs got to work putting fluids into her and wrapping her in the thermal blankets. They added an oxygen mask with warm air to warm up her airways since she seemed to be having a difficult time breathing.

He rode in the back of the ambulance and shot a text off to Logan, telling him what was going on. He made a point to ask Logan to have the police interview Lee and all the workers.

Logan replied that he'd just arrived and that the police had the entire place on lockdown under Barbara's orders, and they were interviewing everyone there. They were looking at the tracks in the snow and checking everyone's boots against the tracks.

"S-S..." Laura lifted her hand towards him.

"Shh," he said softly. "Try not to speak."

She held up her hand again towards him.

He took her cold hand and realized that there was something in it.

"Him," she said and closed her eyes.

With shaky hands, Simon opened the paper Laura had been holding, and read.

I warned you. Get out of my state. Her death is all your fault.

CHAPTER 19

"He can't be that stupid," someone said loudly, causing Laura to pry open her eyes.

"He can and he obviously is," Simon replied.

"There's no proof it was him," someone else said.

"It's my word against his. He's said the very same thing to me several times," Simon replied.

"Did anyone else witness this?" the first person asked.

"No, it was over the phone," Simon answered. "You can check my logs. I called the number he left with my employee."

"This email says the number belongs to a Max Duke," the first person said.

She sighed loudly, getting everyone's attention.

"Hey." Simon's face appeared in front of her eyes. "How are you feeling?"

She quickly assessed her body and realized that everything was numb. Which was better than last time when she'd been frozen, and her skin felt like needles were poking her everywhere.

She shrugged as her answer since her throat was too raw to talk.

"Don't try to talk," Simon warned. "Your family is here." He motioned and suddenly Logan's face appeared above her, then her mother's.

"Hey," both of them said at the same time.

She reached up and took her mother's hand.

"We're here," her mother said. "Rest now. We'll be right here."

Laura closed her eyes again and drifted off into a numbing sleep.

The next time when she woke, the room was dark. Very dark. For a moment, she feared she was back in the garage, then she jerked her hand and felt Simon's in it.

"Hey." He appeared in front of her eyes again. "I'm here."

A low light filled the room. "Your family went home for the night," he said. "They'll be back in the morning."

She tried her voice out and found that even though her throat was raw, she could talk. "I'm sore."

"I can order you some warm tea?" he suggested.

She nodded and he reached down to hit the button on the side of the bed.

"Do you remember what happened?" Simon asked as they waited.

She reached over and hit the button to raise the back of the bed up. When she was sitting up a little, she closed her eyes and tried to play back what had happened.

"I went out to the garage. Someone had told me that there were a few boxes that had been delivered out there. When I got out there, I felt a hand wrap around my throat." She lifted her hand to her throat and realized just why it was sore. "I fought." She closed her eyes. "Or at least I like to think I did. I heard laughter, then… a man whispered in my hear that he had a note he wanted me to give you. He put the paper in my hand and then…" She sighed. "Everything went dark until you were carrying me back inside."

"You didn't see who attacked you?" Simon asked.

"No," she said as she shook her head. "He came at me from behind."

Just then a nurse came in, and Simon requested warm tea.

"The boot prints match a few of the guys on site. It's a standard size and work boot that most of the men wear." Simon sighed. "But I'm pretty sure it was Lee."

Laura frowned. "He's the one who told me about the boxes being delivered to the garage."

Simon sat up. "He was?"

She nodded and Simon smiled. "We got 'em," he said before pulling out his cell phone.

She lay back and closed her eyes as he talked on the phone. She hadn't realized she'd fallen back to sleep until he woke her to tell her that her tea had arrived.

Swallowing the warm liquid, she moaned with delight at the feeling of it warming her further.

"Better?" Simon asked.

"Yes." She cleared her throat and relaxed back. "Thank you."

"Rest," he said, taking her hand in his. "We can finish talking in the morning."

"Crawl in here with me," she suggested, trying to move over in the bed.

He lifted her and laid her on his chest, wrapping his arms around her. "There, better?" he asked.

She pulled the blankets up over her and sighed. "Yes," she said before falling fast asleep listening to his steady heartbeat.

The following morning a tray of warm food was delivered to her just before a young female doctor walked in and gave her a quick checkup. She assured her that, once she was up and walking around, she would be able to go home.

Laura desperately wanted a shower. A very hot one, and her own bed again. One where Simon wrapped himself around her and held onto her all night like he had done the last few nights.

Moments after the doctor left, her mother, Logan, and Amy walked in, each of them carrying large bundles of flowers.

"Sorry, sis. They were out of yellow daisies," Logan said.

It was then that Laura noticed the three dozen daisies that sat on the shelf behind her head.

"From you?" she asked Simon.

He smiled. "I had them delivered." He bent down and kissed her.

"Thank you," she said softly just before she started coughing.

The doctor had told her that her throat would be raw for a few days and to get plenty of warm fluids and to stay silent as much as she could.

"See, doctors' orders," Logan joked. "The medical field even wants you to shut up."

Amy slapped her husband's shoulder playfully.

Laura couldn't help but laugh, which had her coughing even more.

Her mother had brought a bag of clothing for her to change into. After a quick shower, during which she worried numerous times that she would accidentally pull the emergency cord and have someone rushing in to save her naked ass, she dressed in the borrowed clothes and tried to fix her face and hair.

She noticed a deep purple bruise that wrapped around her throat and winced when she touched the spot.

Thankfully, her mother had packed her one of her turtle-neck sweaters.

Her mother's feet were smaller than her own, but she'd brought an old pair of Uggs, which fit Laura perfectly. Thankfully, they were extremely warm.

When she stepped out of the bathroom, Simon glanced up from his phone.

His eyes ran over her and he smiled. "They've arrested Lee," he informed her.

"Good," she said, setting the bag on the end of the bed. "Where did my family go?"

"Home, to our place. Your mom said something about making you lunch, which should be ready by the time we get there."

"I'm so ready to get out of here."

"Sorry, but we have to wait until the police interview you. They said they'd be by this morning."

She sat on the edge of the bed and frowned. "I lost my phone again."

He nodded. "I found it." He pulled a phone from his back pocket. "Sorry, it was smashed, so I had your brother go and replace it this morning." He handed her the new iPhone.

"Twice in one month." She groaned. "I guess it is a good thing I paid for the insurance."

He chuckled. "Yeah, I wish I had done that. I had to pay for my new phone when I lost it in the limo. I did get the insurance this time though." He waved his new phone. "I used to think that insurance was a scam." He chuckled.

She smiled. "It's paid off for me." She glanced down at the phone and smiled when she realized that none of her contacts and data had been lost.

Seeing the pictures of her and Simon smiling with the Christmas tree behind them in Idaho Springs, she realized that no matter how the evening had ended, it was still one of her favorite dates.

"Hey," he said, startling her as he looked over her shoulder. "That's a great picture of us."

"Yeah." She smiled down at it. "I'm thinking of ordering a few prints of it to have framed."

"It would look great over our fireplace."

Just then there was a knock on the door and it swung open.

For the next hour, she answered questions from the female police officer. Some of the questions were personal, such as if she believed she'd been sexually assaulted. She'd instantly said that she hadn't, but a shiver raced through her at the possibility. The man could have done anything to her after he'd knocked her out. Anything.

Simon's arms tightened around her at that moment, and she could tell he was thinking the same.

During the drive back up to the house, she remained silent and watched the new snowfall.

"I'm sorry," she said softly as tears slipped down her face. She dashed them away quickly, not wanting him to see them.

"Don't," he warned. "I don't think I can take your tears."

"I'm sorry," she said again and closed her eyes. "I shouldn't have gone out there alone."

"Hey." He took her hand, and she realized he'd pulled the car over to the side of the road. She turned to him and looked into his eyes. "I should've been there. I'm the reason you're in danger in the first place."

"No, you're not." Her tears dried up slightly. "You have nothing to do with why we're both in danger."

"If I hadn't returned…" he started, but she interrupted him.

"What? Now just because you were born you are responsible for all the stupid things your father is doing?" She felt her anger boil at a man she hadn't even met.

He smiled and she understood instantly that he'd purposely redirected her emotions.

"You did that on purpose." She narrowed her eyes at him.

"You're no longer crying," he pointed out.

She sighed. "I'm upset that I didn't get my work done yesterday," she lied, causing him to chuckle as he pulled back onto the road.

"I was told this morning that it's all finished." He glanced over at her. "The rest of the workers, after hearing what happened to you, worked through the night and this morning to ensure that everything got done."

"It's all…?" She closed her eyes.

"They finished it. Everything," he said with a smile.

"I want to see it."

"You can see it tomorrow," he promised. "Today, we're going to have your mom's home cooking and then snuggle on the sofa and watch a game with your family."

"That sounds amazing," she admitted, and rested her head back.

He was true to his word. For the rest of that day, the only excitement they had was watching the Avalanche win the game.

Her mother made turkey soup with homemade noodles, along with warm freshly baked bread.

He made sure that Laura had enough and enjoyed two full bowls of the soup himself. Logan and Amy had stopped somewhere along the way and had grabbed an apple pie and French vanilla ice cream for dessert, one of Laura's favorites.

He was happily surprised when she ate two whole pieces and then quickly fell asleep on the sofa with her head in his lap.

Her family got the hint and, after the game ended, they left as quietly as they could.

He continued to watch the news on mute until he grew tired, then lifted her into his arms and carried her into their bedroom. She woke up when he laid her on the bed.

"Sorry, I didn't mean to wake you." He sat next to her.

"It's okay." She yawned. "Did my family leave?" She glanced around.

"Yeah, about an hour ago." He reached up to brush her hair

away from her face.

"I must look a mess," she said with a sigh.

He chuckled. "I've seen you looking worse," he promised her.

She frowned up at him. "That's terrible. But true."

He smiled. "I thought tomorrow, after we go and see the facility, that we'd head out and get a tree?"

She sat up slightly and gasped. "A Christmas tree. I… hadn't thought… We need to finish decorating the facility."

"Easy." He touched her shoulder. "Barbara and the crew have taken care of that part. They are all ready for the big party. I was talking about a tree for here." He glanced around. "Maybe we can have two trees. One for the living room and one for in here?"

She relaxed back and smiled. "I'd like that. I have a box of decorations… I think my brother put it in the garage."

"We'll find it. If not, we can always buy more."

"Did they charge Lee?" she asked.

"I haven't heard yet. I expected to get a call sometime today." He glanced down at his phone, which was sitting on the nightstand.

"Do you think he was directed by your father?" she asked.

"The police have the note he left for me to find, which was obviously from him. If he's behind the attack on you, it was sloppy of him. If Lee confesses, the police could have enough on Joseph Wilson to finally lock him up," Simon said, trying not to get his hopes up.

"We can hope." She touched his hand. "I know I've already showered, but it would be nice to use my own shampoo and sit under the hot spray for a while." He helped her stand up. "Care to join me?"

"Do you even have to ask?" He took her hand in his and led them into the bathroom.

"I feel like I'm forever borrowing someone else's clothes," she said as she pulled off her mother's items.

Stepping under the hot spray with Laura in his arms, he realized just how lucky he was. Her arms wrapped around him, and he felt her sigh against his skin.

"I'm so thankful you were there," she said. "I don't know how much longer I could have lasted."

He did. He'd talked to the doctor when she'd been out. From their best guess, Laura had been out in the cold garage for a little over half an hour. When the sun disappeared behind the mountains, cutting off the light and heat to the garage, she would have had only a few more minutes before passing the point of no return. The blanket that had been tossed over her had been to conceal her, not to warm her. The doctor claimed that she was lucky that frostbite hadn't taken any of her fingers.

He felt her shiver and tighten his hold on her. "You okay?" he asked.

She sighed and he knew that she was crying. "Just thinking."

"Don't. You're safe now. Here, with me." He rubbed his hands down her back. "I'm not going to let anything bad happen to you again. I promise." He closed his eyes and took a moment to memorize everything about her.

"I love you," she said softly. "I won't let your father or anyone else tear us apart."

He leaned back and shifted so he could look down into her eyes. "I think it's time I took a stand against him."

"How?"

"I'm supposed to do a news conference on Monday," he said with a slow smile. "I might just let it slip who my family is."

She jerked in his arms and laughed. "That's an amazing idea. You'd be forcing his hand. That way if anything happened to you..."

"Or someone I care about," he added.

"Right." She nodded. "If anything were to happen, it would catch the media's attention."

"Yup." He smiled. "So, we're in agreement?" he asked, liking the plan even more since Laura was okay with it.

"Yes." She nodded. "Now I may have to let you take me shopping this weekend. I don't think I have anything appropriate to wear to a news conference."

He chuckled and wrapped his arms around her again. "Anything you want." He lifted her chin up and placed his lips softly over hers. "Anything," he said again.

He couldn't control his body as she rubbed hers against him.

"Laura," he warned.

"Please, Simon, I need to feel alive," she begged. "I need you."

"Are you up for this?" he asked.

She chuckled. "I've just taken a five-hour nap," she purred as she wrapped her fingers around his growing cock.

He lost all ability to think as she started moving against him. Running his hands slowly over her wet body, he enjoyed the little sexy sounds she was making.

"Please," she practically purred against his skin, "show me. Show me that I'm alive. That you love me."

"I do," he said, lifting her into his arms and sitting on the shower bench. She slid onto his lap, her thighs on either side of his as he adjusted himself into her. As she slid slowly down on him, he kissed her and held her tight. She felt so right in his arms, felt so right in his life.

He knew that it wasn't his fault his father was a power-hungry megalomaniac. And no matter what happened now, he wasn't going to let the man ruin his life again. Not when he had finally just won Laura back.

"I love you," he said as she slumped against him after their mutual release. "Marry me. Be with me. Always."

She leaned back, tears rolling down her cheeks and a smile on her lips.

"Yes, of course, I will. Always," she said before kissing him.

They sat under the hot spray until Laura sighed, and he knew that she was tired again. Then he lit another fire in the bedroom, and they crawled under the covers. When he heard her stomach growl, he went into the kitchen and grabbed the rest of the pie. They sat up in bed watching a Hallmark Christmas special until she fell back to sleep in his arms. He thought about the ring and the other gifts he'd purchased for her, which were still locked in his glove box.

The following morning, they woke to a fresh foot of snow. Laura seemed to be in a better mood and, as far as he could tell, she was physically back to normal.

They dressed and, after eating the breakfast of French toast and eggs they'd made together, he drove them down to the facility.

He'd sent a text to Barbara to let her know they would be stopping by and when they walked in, all of the staff were waiting for them.

The front hall was completely decorated for the holiday. A massive Christmas tree and faux red Santa sleigh were set up in the main entryway. String lights and fake snow were every-where, along with other images of the holiday.

"Welcome back," everyone cheered as they entered.

Laura laughed and hugged everyone, and they all wished her a speedy recovery.

He was happily surprised to see how much the staff knew and cared for Laura. Barbara even cried a little when Laura replayed what had happened to her.

"I should have known that man was no good," Barbara said. "I saw him sneaking around in the basement the other day."

"You did?" he asked. "Where?"

"The boiler rooms. I thought maybe he was helping the guys check the system out, but now…" She dropped off.

Laura looked at him. "What's wrong?" she asked.

"Nothing," he lied and thought about heading down there to make sure the man hadn't damaged anything. "I…" He stopped when she took his hand in his.

"We'll check it out together," she said softly. "After this party is over."

He nodded. "I'll call the HVAC guys in to check the system as well." He pulled out his phone and shot a text message off to the head HVAC contractor, Wayne. After getting an instant reply from the man, who said he was already on site, he suggested they all head down there now.

The heavy metal door that led to the basement area had a new lock that could only be unlocked by a staff member's key card or a code. Simon used his master key card and led Laura down the metal flight of stairs into the massive basement.

The old basement had been cleared out and now housed a large room of computer servers that ran the entire facility, a large storage room that was currently half-empty, and three smaller storage rooms that were full of donated clothing and children items. Then there was the massive HVAC room that housed almost all of the building's brand new heating and air-conditioning systems, along with the boiler for the hot water. There were two massive fans on the roof of the building that had been helicoptered into place during construction.

Seeing Wayne and a few of his workers, they made their way across the basement.

"What about the other rooms?" Laura asked, nodding towards the closed doors to the storage areas.

"We'll check them too," he agreed. After shaking Wayne's hand, he explained his concerns about Lee being seen down there a few days ago.

"My guys have been working down here nonstop. We've made the necessary changes to the system since it's been up and running for the past forty-eight hours." He nodded towards the room that housed most of the system. "She's purring like a Jaguar." The man smiled with pride. "We haven't seen anything off in here."

"Good." Simon relaxed slightly. "We'll go check the other rooms then."

Taking Laura's hand, he unlocked the first storage room and turned on the bright lights.

"Wow, I can't believe how much stuff was donated. I saw a few loads of this being delivered." Laura stepped into the room. "The kids are going to love picking out their own clothes." She turned around and took everything in. "You know, I could help down here too. Maybe set it up like a closet or a store?" she suggested. She tilted her head, as if she was thinking. "You know, arrange everything by age, size, sex." She shrugged and looked at him.

"That would be… wonderful." He smiled and walked over to hug her.

"And this is just one room?" she asked.

"Yeah." He motioned towards the other two small rooms. "Three rooms. I had the staff separate it out by age. This is infant through toddler. Next door is toddler through pre-teen and the last…"

"Is teen and up," she replied with a smile. "Smart. I think with some racks in here, the kids would feel like they're going shopping instead of getting handouts."

"Great idea," he agreed.

"We could even paint the walls…" she started, and he chuckled.

"I get it. You'll have free rein down here when you're up to it." He laughed when she did a little buggy dance.

"This is going to be so much fun." She laughed and hugged him again.

His smile fell away as he realized that nothing in the room had been disturbed. "Let's try the next room."

The moment he unlocked the next door, he knew instantly that there was something wrong.

CHAPTER 21

She knew there was something wrong when she felt Simon tense next to her.

"What is it?" she asked at the same moment that he pushed her body behind his.

"Run!" he screamed and slammed the door shut just as the explosion sent her flying backwards. Her body hit the cement wall a few feet away, knocking the breath out of her and causing her head to spin.

"Run!" Simon's cry echoed in her head. Everything was fuzzy for a moment and seemed to pulse with each heartbeat.

She could hear the workers that they'd just talked to yelling and watched as they ran towards her as if in slow motion. There was so much yelling and she tried to focus on what was being said, but there was a high-pitched ringing in her hears from the explosion.

"Grab the fire extinguisher!" someone shouted.

"Put it out! Smother it!" someone else was shouting.

Simon, she thought and glanced around for him. Wayne and another man were huddled, working over a figure and spraying the area with a fire extinguisher.

She turned her attention back towards the doorway. The explosion had almost ripped the door off the hinges, and she watched in horror as several of the men battled a fire that had broken out inside the room after the initial explosion.

Everything, all of the donated clothes for the young kids, was on fire.

"Get her out of here," she heard Simon's voice finally.

"Simon!" she cried and tried to crawl towards his voice. It was then that she noticed he'd been the one on fire. The one Wayne and the other guy had been trying to rescue. "Simon," she cried again when she noticed the burns on his hands and arms. His sweater was ripped completely off, and she could clearly see his red skin covered in a layer of foam from the fire extinguisher. Wayne had used a fire blanket to put out the fire that had taken most of his clothes. The blanket covered most of Simon's body.

"Get her out of here," Simon said to Wayne. "In case there's another bomb." He pushed the man with his burned hand.

"Sorry about this," Wayne said to her as he scooped her up in his arms and rushed up the stairs.

"What's happened?" Barbara met them at the top of the stairs.

"Bomb," Wayne said quickly. "Call—"

"They're on their way," Barbara finished. "We've evacuated the building. Here, take her outside."

Wayne followed Barbara outside into the snow.

"Simon," she cried. "Wayne, go back and get him."

"My guys are bringing him out now." He motioned towards the doors.

It seemed to take forever as she watched and waited for the front doors of the building to open. Finally, moments later, two guys came running out of the building with Simon hobbling between them, holding onto their shoulders.

"We've got the fire out, boss," one of the men said to Wayne.

"We'll wait for the bomb squad to clear the building. Is everyone out?" Wayne asked.

"Yeah, we're the last," one of the guys who held up Simon said.

"Laura?" Simon reached for her.

"I'm okay," she cried and hobbled over to wrap her arms around him. "My god," she cried as she held onto him. "I was so afraid."

"I almost lost you. That son of a bitch," Simon growled. "I've had enough of this."

They both jerked as the fire truck stopped next to them. They stood back as the crew jumped into action.

Another car squealed to a stop, and Logan and Amy rushed to her side to gather them both in their arms.

"We were driving by and saw the fire trucks. What happened?" Amy said, then she gasped. "You're burned," she said to Simon.

"Just singed." He glanced down at his arms and hands. "Thanks to Wayne." He nodded to the man who was standing there talking to the fire chief, telling him that the fire was out but that it had been a bomb. The chief recalled his crew and told them they would wait for the bomb squad do a sweep and clear the building.

They were pulled by Logan towards a waiting ambulance. She made a point to have them check on Simon first. They treated the first-degree burns to his hands and arms that he'd gotten when he'd shut the door during the explosion.

She was pretty sure that if he hadn't shut the door like he had, the fire would have ravaged through the entire facility. Then again, that was probably their plan. Simon had been quick to shut the door. Someone else might not have been. The explosion would have traveled down the hallway and caused more damage than what she remembered seeing. Where they just trying to cause damage? To shake Simon up? Looking at him now, she realized that if that had been the purpose, they had hit the mark. He was obviously very upset.

"I would like to stay," Simon was telling the EMT.

"No, we'll go." She touched Simon's shoulder. "You need to be checked out. The police are going to clear the building. We can't go in now anyway." When he opened his mouth to argue, she reached up and touched her head. "Besides, I'm seeing double and might need another CT scan."

That did the trick. He finally agreed to ride in the back of the ambulance to the hospital.

"This time I'm going to leave here in my own clothes," she warned as they wheeled them inside.

Simon's chuckle in response was one of the best sounds in the world. They treated Simon's burns while she waited to be rolled in for another scan.

An hour after arriving at the ER, Logan walked in and informed them that the facility had been cleared and that the damage had been contained to the one storage room.

"Unfortunately, everything inside was destroyed," Logan added. "The other storage areas were untouched."

"Thankfully," Amy added. "They've also confirmed that there wasn't any structural damage."

"That's good news." Laura sighed and relaxed. "Hopefully, this won't push back the opening?"

"What about the safety of the children?" Amy asked. "If this is your father, like Logan has suggested, what if Lee Cummings isn't the only one working for the senator?"

The room grew silent.

"I'm going to step up security," Simon said with a sigh. "Shit, maybe I should distance myself from the facility?"

"No." Laura shook her head, then turned to her brother. "How fast can you get the press here?" she said with a thought, then turned to Simon. "I think we need to step up our timeline.

We have to fight fire with fire. We can't have him hiding in the shadows anymore."

"That's an idea," Simon agreed.

"It might go a long way to mention the bombing. Maybe twist it like someone was out to hurt you and the senator?" Logan thought out loud. "The man is an egotistical maniac. If you portray it as someone trying to hurt him through you, your father could portray the situation as if someone is out to hurt him by hurting you. You know, he could play the victim."

"What if he decides he likes that victim role and continues to try and hurt you?" Amy asked.

"Something tells me he won't," Simon replied as he glanced down at his bandaged hands.

"How are you doing, sis?" Logan asked her.

"Clean bill of health. We're just waiting for the okay to leave," she answered.

"They aren't keeping you here overnight?" Amy asked.

"No." Laura shook her head and glanced over at Simon. "We're going home tonight."

"After we go and check out the damage at the facility," Simon added. "And stop off and pick up a Christmas tree."

Laura shook her head. "Simon, we can do that—"

"Today," he said. "I'm not going to let that man ruin one more day of ours."

"We can help you with the tree," Logan added. "You'll need it now that your hands are out of commission for a while."

Simon glanced down at his bandaged hands and sighed. "They aren't that bad. But we'd appreciate it."

"Good, it's settled then." Amy smiled. "Dinner at your place while we decorate your home. I'll call Gina and have her meet us there."

A little over an hour later, they stood in the same spot they had when the explosion knocked them around.

The charred remains of everything that sat in the room had Laura's eyes tearing up.

"Things can be replaced," Simon said, wrapping his arm around her.

"I'm not crying for the items. It could have been so much worse." She looked at the damaged door that hung off the hinges. "If you hadn't shut the door…"

"Yeah," Simon said with a sigh. "Yeah." He shook his head. "I'm thankful I reacted as fast as I did."

"How did you know?" she asked him.

"I smelled the petrol. There was a strong odor of it long before I saw the gas cans and the timer. The smell had me on guard," he said. "I wish I'd smelled it in the hallway long before I opened the door, but…" He shrugged.

"I'm thankful you did." She hugged him.

"Boss," Barbara called out. "The press is here."

Simon glanced down at her. They had rushed home from the hospital and changed out of their destroyed clothes. Her mother had asked to be let in so she could start prepping dinner.

"Ready?" Simon said, taking her hand in his bandaged one.

"Yes." She smiled up at him.

She stood by Simon's side in the front lobby in front of the beautiful Christmas display. As she listened to Simon talk to the press, she realized that she loved him more now than she had ever loved him. It was as if the five years they'd been apart had melted away.

He'd come back to her a better man. A stronger man. One that she loved more than she'd ever believed she could.

"Thank you, everyone, for coming down here on such short notice. I know we had this scheduled for Monday, but with today's events, I felt it was better to quash any questions and concerns you may have now," Simon started.

Several questions were thrown at him by the press, but Simon held up his hands.

"I will take questions after I make my statement. First, I want to assure everyone that ReNewed Foster Care Facility will be opening our doors officially on the twenty-third. Security is my and my staff's number one priority, and we've tripled our efforts to ensure the safety of our facility and everyone inside. With that said, today's incident has caused a need for more donations. We're looking to replace the items damaged." He glanced down at the sheet of paper Barbara had handed to him and rattled off the age groups and items they were in need of. Then he set the paper aside and took a deep breath. "The next course of business is a little more personal. There have been rumors going around about my family life." He glanced at Laura and smiled. "It's true that I was raised in the foster care program here in Colorado. I'm thankful for the love and care I received growing up and want to ensure that other children are as lucky as I was. However, what isn't known is that I found out a few years back who my biological parents were. My mother, Grace Renee Rodgers died in an incident shortly after I was given up for adoption. My father"—Simon paused to take a deep breath—"is very familiar to most of those living in the state— Joseph Wilson."

It seemed to take a heartbeat for the name to sink in. Then more questions were thrown at Simon as the sounds of cameras filled the silence.

Simon again held up his hands to quiet everyone.

"Yes, the senator knows who I am. I found him a little over five years ago, shortly after my records were unsealed on my eighteenth birthday. No, my father and I haven't seen one another since that day. I am sure, however, that he is just as eager to ensure ReNewed's safe opening since he saw fit to ensure the well-being of so many children in foster care. I know I have benefited from several of the laws he has put in place over the years for kids in dangerous situations like those I grew up in."

Laura smiled and felt a rush of pride flood her. Simon was a genius. She hadn't even thought of taking that angle. She glanced up at him with love and pride as he finished twisting his father's destructive laws, which he'd signed over the years.

"The last bit of news is even more personal." He reached over and took her hand in his. She gently held onto it since she noticed him wince with pain. "I'd like to officially announce my engagement to the love of my life, Laura Miller. Laura and her family have always been there for me throughout the years, and I can't wait to officially become part of their family." He wrapped his arms around her and kissed her while the cameras snapped more pictures.

CHAPTER 22

"*D*id you hear all those questions?" Laura said as she drove his car back to their house. "So many were about the explosion and tying your father to the worker Lee Cummings." She smiled quickly over at him.

"Yeah, something tells me the press isn't as dumb as my father likes to portray them." Simon chuckled. He was feeling like he was at the end of his strength.

He would have liked to pick out his and Laura's first Christmas tree together but was thankful Logan and Amy had volunteered to pick one up for them instead.

At this rate, he doubted he would be able to keep his eyes open to help decorate the thing. He loved the holiday season, he really did, but after everything he'd been through in the past month and a half, he just wanted some peace and quiet for a while.

There was less than a week before the facility would start filling with children and now the entire building had to be reinspected thanks to the bomb. Sure, the bomb squad and the fire department had cleared the damage as minimal, but he knew that the state would need another inspection before they signed off on children being moved into the facility.

Which meant more work for him and his crew. The door to the damaged storage room had to be replaced, the destroyed items hauled out, and the room repainted. Laura had talked eagerly about it on the trip home.

Stepping into the house and smelling the food that Gina had cooked mixed with the distinct scent of pine tree, he felt the last hold on his emotions slip.

Pulling Laura into his arms, he held onto her and tried to take it all in, tried to hold onto the moment as long as he could.

"Everything okay?" Gina asked.

"Yeah." He sighed and kissed Laura. "It is now." He reached over and grabbed Gina up and pulled her into the hug.

Laura's mother easily wrapped her arms around the pair of them. "We caught your little show." She laughed and kissed him on the cheek. "Welcome to the family."

He smiled. "Which reminds me." He glanced at Laura. "I forgot something out in the car."

She handed him the keys.

"I'll be right back." He raced back out into the snow. When he came back, the small box tucked in his pocket and the rest of the gifts ready to go under the tree, everyone in the room was gathered around the tree that Logan had set up next to the windows.

"It's bigger than ours," Amy said with a chuckle. "It's a good thing your living room is taller than ours as well."

"I figured you would want something big enough to fill the space here by the windows," Logan said with a smile.

"It's perfect," Laura said, wrapping her arm around his waist.

"What do you say we eat dinner, then decorate this beast?" Gina asked. "I've cooked us a proper Christmas feast since I wasn't sure we'd be able to do this again next week, with the party and all going on. Besides, we're celebrating today."

"I love it. It sounds like a perfect end to a crazy day," he said, knowing that it was perfect timing.

Sitting around the dining table, in the freshly painted room, he realized he'd been a fool all those years ago.

He should have never looked for his birth parents. Not when he had such a great family right in front of him all along. If he had just stayed the course, he could have held onto everything that was dear to him from the start.

After stuffing his face with turkey, ham, and all the fixings of a full holiday meal, he could barely keep his eyes open.

They moved into the living area where he watched his family start to decorate the massive tree.

Amy had purchased several boxes of white lights, which were quickly wrapped around the tree and plugged in. As far as the ornaments went, however, they didn't have enough to fill the massive tree. It was decided that they would fill the front of the tree and leave the back empty.

By the time everyone was done hanging the last ornament, his eyelids were extremely heavy, and he kept nodding off. The game was put on the television, which only increased his drowsiness by filling the room with the soothing sounds of the sports he loved.

He listened to everyone chatting while the dishes were done as he drifted off.

"Simon?" Laura shook him awake later. "We thought you'd want to see this." She motioned towards the television. "It's your father. He's about to make a statement."

He blinked a few times as he sat up, wincing when he forgot about the burns on his hands and tried to use them to sit up.

"Easy," Laura said as she helped him sit up.

The television sound was turned up and, sure enough, his father's face suddenly filled the screen.

"Wow, you do look like him," Logan said under his breath. "You have the same eyes."

"Yeah, it's a kicker," Simon said.

"Tell me about it. I'm a spitting image of my old man. Good thing the SOB is dead," Logan added with a frown.

Everyone grew quiet as his father started speaking.

"I'd like to address the rumors of my infidelity and that I fathered a child twenty-some years ago…"

"Twenty-three," Simon added dryly. "But he probably doesn't even know that."

"I adamantly deny any such rumors," he finished.

Immediately, questions were shouted out at him with one reporter's voice ringing out over the rest.

"How do you explain Simon Berg's birth certificate that shows you as the biological father?"

The senator didn't even respond to the questions thrown at him and continued to talk over everyone.

"I would be happy to take a DNA test, proving my point. As to ensuring that the ReNewed facility's doors open, I have never interfered with any business in all my years as your state senator, and I assure you, I have done nothing but ensure the well-being and safety of young at-risk children."

There was a large scuffle as reporters turned away from the senator while a whisper of something circulated through the crowd. Immediately, the camera changed to show the local news anchor, who looked extremely surprised.

"What's going on?" Simon sat up.

"We are just getting word," the news anchor said, "that Senator Joseph Wilson is being arrested on attempted kidnapping charges and conspiracy to commit arson. We are now going to the local police chief, who is holding a news briefing on this subject."

The screen changed back to the same podium where the senator, who was now being cuffed, had been standing moments before.

"…with the latest proof, we are taking Senator Joseph Wilson into custody effective immediately and he is being charged with…" The man looked down at the paper in front of him. "The kidnapping of Laura Miller and conspiracy to commit arson for the bombing and fire that happened earlier today at the ReNewed Foster Care Facility in Golden. We have substantial proof that Mr. Wilson was involved in both instances, thanks to items Lee Cummings has provided. Mr. Cummings has been on Senator Wilson's payroll for more than six years. He was identified as a man of interest posing as a city permit worker and is himself being charged with a break-in and property destruction to a property on Indian Paintbrush Drive, which he claims he'd mixed up the addresses and believed was the residence of Simon Berg. He's also responsible for the hit-and-run that sent Mr. Berg and Laura Miller's limo careening off the road into Clear Creek. That crash resulted in the death of limo driver, a single mother named Kayla Smith, who left behind a two-year-old daughter, who is now safely in her grandmother's custody."

He reached for Laura's hand. "She has a family." He felt the tears sting his eyes.

"He was the one who pushed us off the road?" Laura asked as an image of Lee Cummings flashed on the screen.

"He broke into the Anderson's home," Amy said softly with a shiver.

Simon felt his anger spike. If he had known they'd allowed a murderer to work at his facility, he would have…

"Easy," Laura said softly. "We couldn't have known it was him before now."

"I let him into my facility." He practically growled it as the police chief continued to talk in the background.

"You couldn't have known," Logan agreed.

"I'm going to do everything in my power to make sure this doesn't happen again. No one is going to step foot in that facility without a full background check," he added with something close to a growl.

"Good idea," Gina said with a smile. "But there's no use beating yourself up for past mistakes."

They all grew quiet again while the police chief continued to talk about how Lee Cummings was cooperating and willing to testify that he'd been hired by the senator to take down Simon Berg and anyone close to him before he could expose his relationship to the senator. The chief went on to explain how two other parties had come forward and claimed they are the senator's children, a Rosaline Sanders, who was twenty-two, and a Shane Wallis, age eighteen.

"I have a brother and sister," Simon said, feeling his heart skip in his chest.

"Guess his secrets are out now," Laura said softly.

"There's no returning from something like that," Logan agreed. "Not only did he lie, but he also tried to kill to cover it up."

"No, there's no returning from that," Simon agreed. "Being cuffed at your own news conference." He smiled and glanced over at Laura. "That's the best present I could have asked for. Knowing that my family will be safe from that madman."

"You're the best gift I could have asked for," Laura said before she kissed him.

"Speaking of gifts." He pulled out the small box. "We haven't made this official yet." He slid off the sofa and knelt before her. "I wanted to give you flowers and... well"—he glanced at his bandaged hands—"a fully functional man, but this will have to do. Laura, will you marry me?"

"Yes." Her smile grew as she pulled him close and hugged him. "Of course, I will." She kissed him.

He watched her face as she opened the ring box and saw more tears fill her eyes. "It's perfect," she said as he slid it onto her finger.

"This calls for a toast," Gina said, getting their attention. He'd almost forgotten that the rest of her family was still there.

Logan disappeared into the kitchen and brought back a bottle of champagne and poured a glass for everyone except for Amy, who held up her bottle of water.

"To family." Simon held up his glass and toasted. "May it grow in size and love."

*L*aura stood back and watched Simon, dressed in a large white beard and padded belly, hand out the carefully wrapped presents to each child as they approached his spot on the sleigh.

She had to admit that Simon was the sexiest Santa Claus she'd ever seen. The sexiest and the best one. He knew each child by name. She already knew that each present was exactly what each child had asked for. How he had found that bit of news out was still a mystery. He wouldn't tell her how he'd obtained that knowledge. Every time she'd asked him, he'd just told her he had an 'in' with the big man.

Even the teenagers seemed to enjoy getting in the spirit. It tickled her to see Kevin, a young boy roughly twelve-years-old, complete with his tall purple mohawk, sit in the sleigh next to Simon and wrap his arm around Santa's shoulders to smile for a picture.

Laura had spent the last few days getting to know each child and could tell that she was going to have a difficult time turning over several to the new families that were waiting in line to host or adopt the kids.

"It just makes you want to adopt them all, doesn't it?" her mother said, wrapping an arm around Laura's shoulders.

"Yes," she admitted with a sigh. "I can tell already that we're going to need a bigger house." She chuckled. She thought of the gift she'd finally given Simon that morning, which hung over their fireplace proudly. Now anyone who walked into their home would see the history of their relationship.

"I'm thinking of taking that boy myself." Her mother nodded towards Kevin. "I've spent some time with him over the past few days." She turned to her. "Did you know he can play classical piano like a pro?"

"No." Laura glanced at Kevin again and then laughed. "I guess looks can be deceiving."

"Yeah, he's a sweet kid. His parents were killed about a year ago in a drunk-driving accident. His father played in a punk band." Her mother smiled. "His dad taught him how to play several instruments, and he fell in love with playing the piano quickly."

Laura turned to her mother.

"Do you think you can handle another kid? I mean, after Logan you always said..." She laughed when Logan pinched her arm.

"What did you say?" Logan asked their mother.

Not missing a beat, she replied. "That I'd happily have another dozen just like the pair of you."

Laura laughed.

"I think you and Kevin would get along famously," she admitted.

"I've got my first grandchild on the way and, well, I've realized my place is empty," she said with a shrug. "Besides, I have that baby grand piano left over since neither of the two of you would touch the thing."

"Neither of us has an ounce of talent... musically," Logan supplied.

"It's true," Laura agreed. "Simon requested that I stop singing Christmas carols earlier today."

Their mother laughed and then sighed as she looked over to where Simon was holding a small child on his lap, talking softly to the girl as she opened her present.

"He sure did come around, didn't he?" she asked.

"Yeah." Logan slung his arm around Laura's and their mother's shoulders. "I guess it was a good thing he had us to set him straight."

Laura laughed. "He's the one who set us straight," she reminded them.

"Yeah," the two of them agreed in unison.

"It's all he ever wished for," Laura added. "To have us as his family."

"Now he has us. Well, next spring when you two make it official, he will," Logan added.

"Yeah." She smiled as Simon locked eyes with her, then wiggled his gloved finger at her.

"Gotta go, I'm being summoned by the big man." She walked across the room and climbed into the sleigh next to Simon.

"There you are, Mrs. Claus," Simon said with a smile.

"Hey now, we haven't made it official yet." She leaned back away from the kiss he was trying to plant on her lips.

"Soon enough," he promised. "Then I'll have everything I've ever wished for." He pulled her into a kiss, and everyone around them cheered.

The Pride Series

Finding Pride

Discovering Pride

Returning Pride

Lasting Pride

Serving Pride

Red Hot Christmas

My Sweet Valentine

Return To Me

Rescue Me

A Pride Christmas

The Secret Series

Secret Seduction

Secret Pleasure

Secret Guardian

Secret Passions

Secret Identity

Secret Sauce

The West Series

Loving Lauren

Taming Alex

Holding Haley

Missy's Moment

Breaking Travis

Roping Ryan

Wild Bride

Corey's Catch

Tessa's Turn

Saving Trace

The Grayton Series

Last Resort

Someday Beach

Rip Current

In Too Deep

Swept Away

High Tide

Lucky Series

Unlucky In Love

Sweet Resolve

Best of Luck

A Little Luck

Christmas Wish

Silver Cove Series

Silver Lining

French Kiss

Happy Accident

Hidden Charm

A Silver Cove Christmas

Sweet Surrender

Entangled Series – Paranormal Romance

The Awakening

The Beckoning

The Ascension

The Presence

The Calling

Haven, Montana Series

Closer to You

Never Let Go

Holding On

Coming Home

Pride Oregon Series

A Dash of Love

My Kind of Love

Season of Love

Tis the Season

Dare to Love

Where I Belong

Because of Love

A Thing Called Love

First Comes Love

Someone to Love

Wildflowers Series

Summer Nights

Summer Heat

Summer Secrets

Summer Fling

Summer's End

Summer's Wish

Distracted Series

Wake Me

Tame Me

Stand Alone Books

Twisted Rock

Hope Harbor

Raven Falls

For a complete list of books:

http://JillSanders.com

ABOUT THE AUTHOR

Jill Sanders is a New York Times, USA Today, and international bestselling author of Sweet Contemporary Romance, Romantic Suspense, Western Romance, and Paranormal Romance novels. With over 70 books in eleven series, translations into several different languages, and audiobooks there's plenty to choose from. Look for Jill's bestselling stories wherever romance books are sold or visit her at jillsanders.com

Jill comes from a large family with six siblings, including an identical twin. She was raised in the Pacific Northwest and later relocated to Colorado for college and a successful IT career before discovering her talent for writing sweet and sexy page-turners. After Colorado, she decided to move south, living in Texas and now making her home along the Emerald Coast of Florida. You will find that the settings of several of her series are inspired by her time spent living in these areas. She has two sons and off-set the testosterone in her house by adopting three furry little ladies that provide her company while she's locked in her writing cave. She enjoys heading to the beach, hiking, swimming, wine-tasting, and pickleball with her husband, and of course writing. If you have read any of her books, you may also notice that there is a

www.ingramcontent.com/pod-product-compliance
Lightning Source LLC
Chambersburg PA
CBHW050407190726
48284CB00007BB/2467